WENDY M. WILSON

A Dark and Painful Mystery

This book was professionally typeset on Reedsy.
Find out more at reedsy.com

Contents

1

Supposed Foul Play

Mysterious Disappearance and Supposed Foul Play

Being so near home as when last heard of, with a straight metalled road all the way, it is impossible to account for his [Peter Kane's] disappearance, and for that reason, the supposition of his being lost in the bush is out of the question. We certainly think the case is one which calls for the strictest investigation, so that the fate of the poor fellow may be cleared up, and the state of horrible suspense in which his unfortunate wife has been kept in for months brought to an end; and we would ask not only the people of Woodville, but of the other districts he may have visited, to take all possible steps to throw light upon what at present appears to be a dark and painful mystery.

The Manawatu Times, Volume III, Issue 81, 20 July 1878

And now, read how Frank and Mette Hardy investigate the disappearance of Peter Kane and the murder of George Ollandt while learning a few things about marriage, loyalty, and their own relationship while they do so.

Note that this book and six others in the series are available as audiobooks on Audible, Apple, Google Play, Chirp, and in some cases, your local library.

To discover other books the series, follow me on BookBub or check my website at www.wendymwilson.com

2

At the Farm

Mette Hardy had imagined her future husband leaning against the mantel, pipe in hand, talking to her about serious matters - books and music, philosophy perhaps. She had imagined herself sitting on a sofa in the parlour darning his socks, listening intently while he expounded on his ideas, and trying hard to learn everything she could. When he had finished speaking he would give her a chance to express her own thoughts, and not smile at what she said, but give her ideas serious consideration. Or at least act as if he did.

Instead, she had Frank, up to his knees in mud, trying to wrestle a tree stump from the ground, his face red with exertion, grunting like a wild pig, and cursing like the soldier he had once been, while she watched him, laughing.

How strange it was that she preferred the husband she had so much more than the one she had imagined. If only he was a little more...well, civilized. She wished he would read a book occasionally, or take her into Palmerston to see a lecture or a concert at Forrester's Hall.

"Could you give me a hand here, Mette? I can't move the bloody thing."

"What can I do?"

"See that plank?"

"This one?"

He nodded. "When I lift the stump, shove the plank underneath it and stand on it. Use that rock for leverage. I'll keep pushing. Between us, we can move it."

The stump rose gradually from the ground and flipped on its side. Frank fell to his knees beside it.

"Thank God for that. I thought I'd never get it out. Thanks for your...look at you. Your skirt's all muddy."

Mette sat down beside him. "I don't care. I like mud. I can grow things in mud."

He pulled her towards him, leaving a muddy handprint on her sleeve. "It suits you."

"You know, when Pieter built his house in the clearing he burned the tree stumps."

"I don't like all the smoke or the ash that ends up in the paddock. Some ash is good, but too much clogs up the grass. Not good for the horses either."

She looked around. "But we don't have any horses."

"We will," he said. "As soon as this paddock's cleared. And when I get some cash in. I'm a bit short right now." He ran his fingers through his hair, leaving a trail of mud along the top. "I may have to look for work."

"I could go back to the book shop."

"Wouldn't you rather work in your garden? I hate the idea of sending you out to work, especially when you make so little. I'd have to take you into Palmerston and wait around...all for a few shillings a week..."

She sighed. She loved her garden, but she'd loved working at the book shop as well. So near to all those books. She wished Frank understood how important reading was to her. For Frank to find work that paid a decent amount, he'd have to leave the farm, and she'd be by herself a mile from the nearest neighbour and fifteen miles from Feilding, the nearest town. "Is there any work you could get nearby?"

"Shearing, I suppose, but it's mostly over, except for the dipping...and harvesting's done as well."

"Would those jobs pay well?"

He wiped his hands on the grass and shook his head. "Not really. There are so many men tramping around the countryside, willing to work for low wages. I suppose the sawmills...I could speak to Richter..."

Mette put her head on his shoulder. "That's not your kind of work. Scandies work at the sawmills"

"Work is work," said Frank. "I'm not too proud to do an honest day's labour in a sawmill."

"Well, let's forget about it for now." Mette lifted the basket she'd carried from the soddy. "I brought you lunch. I made bread, and Maren sent me over some of her cheese and butter. And I picked runner beans from my garden this morning."

He stood and held out his hand to her. "Lunch it is. But I have something to show you - up in the high paddock. Let's have a picnic up there."

He took the basket and she followed him up the track to the high paddock, a mostly grassy area concealed in a dip above the small sod house they were living in temporarily while Frank built a permanent home. The high paddock had a ridge on the near side, facing the house, and Frank had already marked it as a place to hide if they were ever attacked. Not that he expected to be attacked, but, as she'd discovered, he always thought strategically, like the soldier he'd once been.

They reached the high paddock and he pointed to the ridge, where a seat had been hollowed out and lined with logs. She sat beside him and looked at the view of the river winding its way through the landscape in the distance; further away, she could see smoke rising from Feilding chimneys.

"So pretty..."

"We can come up here in the evenings and watch the sunset," said Frank. "Bring a glass of beer - ginger beer for you..."

"That sounds nice." She opened the basket and handed him some bread and cheese. A slight breeze came off the river and she could feel the moisture in the air. She could hardly believe how happy she was.

He stopped eating and cocked his head to one side. "What was that? I heard a whistle."

"It was a bird, I think..."

Frank hopped up on the seat, conveniently located so that the back was at chest height, giving him a good place to rest a rifle if it ever came to that. "It's Karira. He has someone with him." He whistled and waved towards the house.

"Maybe he has a job for you. Wouldn't that be wonderful?"

Constable Karira, late of the Maori Constabulary, had formed a partnership with Frank offering investigations, but the business, which had never really been successful, had died off since Frank had bought himself a farm. Karira kept busy helping the people from his village who had been dispossessed after the chief sold the land to the government.

They hurried down the track to the farmyard. Constable Karira was accompanied by another man, mid-thirties, smartly dressed in a dark suit and straw hat. The men dismounted to greet Frank and Mette.

"Frank, this is Mr. Tomlinson. He manages Beaven's store in Sandon. He has a request."

Frank raised his eyebrows questioningly at Mr. Tomlinson.

"As Constable Karira says, I manage a store in Sandon," said Tomlinson. "One of my regular customers is an Irish woman named Mrs. Kane - Mrs. Mary Kane. She has three young children and she buys milk from me almost every day, in exchange for eggs. I realized recently that I hadn't seen her for several days and stopped by her home to see if there was a problem. People get sick, and..."

"She was sick?" Frank sounded impatient; Mette squeezed his elbow gently. Mr. Tomlinson had a story to tell, and it seemed best to let him tell it his own way.

"Not sick, exactly," said Tomlinson, "Weak from lack of food. She and her three children were sleeping on the floor of the house. She'd sold all her furniture and any spare clothing she had, and they had very little food. Just the last of her seed potatoes—she'd eaten most of them."

"Oh dear," said Mette. "Eating her seed potatoes? The poor woman." You could survive on seed potatoes, but then you'd have nothing to plant for the next year.

"Is there a Mr. Kane?" asked Frank.

Tomlinson nodded. "He left in May last year to find work. He wrote to her several times. The last letter arrived a few weeks before the end of the year. He said he was on his way home and would be in Sandon by Christmas."

Mette gazed at Frank, imagining herself in the same situation. "He's been away from home for almost a year. How can she...?"

"And no contact for four months," said Frank. "What's she done about finding him?"

"She sent a letter to one of the papers in Hawke's Bay, asking them to run an advertisement, but she had no way of knowing if it ran," said Tomlinson. "After I discovered her situation I placed some ads as well, asking people to write to me at the store, but had no response."

"And the police?" asked Frank.

"They searched for him but found nothing. What I was hoping, Sergeant Hardy, was that you could follow in his footsteps and see what you could learn...if anything."

Mette could see that Frank was interested, but she wanted to make sure he would be paid. "How would Mrs. Kane be able to pay for Frank's services? Isn't she destitute?"

"I took up a subscription for her," said Tomlinson. I've raised almost a hundred pounds...people have been very generous."

"Doesn't she need that money?"

"She does, but unfortunately she's refusing to take more than the smallest part of it. She says she prefers to take care of her family herself. I found her work cleaning hotel rooms in the morning, which is all she knows how to do. She leaves the children with a neighbour, but makes barely enough to feed the four of them..."

"The poor woman," said Mette again. Her heart was breaking over the situation in which Mrs. Kane found herself.

"How long do you want me to search for him?" asked Frank. "He's probably lost in the bush somewhere. No use looking forever. If I can't find him in a week or so I'm not going to find him."

"We - my fellow subscribers and I - thought we'd hire you for ten days and we're willing to pay you fifty pounds, whether you find him or not. And another ten for your expenses. I have a mare I'd like to give you as well - I don't have time to breed her and wanted to send her to a good home. Would that suit you?"

"What do you think, Mette? I hate to leave you by yourself for that long... could you stay with your sister?"

"She could stay in town," said Karira, who had been watching the discussion silently. "And I could come out here every few days and keep an eye on the farm."

"Now wait a minute," said Mr. Tomlinson. "I have a better idea." He turned to Mette, his hands clasped in front of his face. "Mrs. Hardy, you seem to be a strong, sympathetic woman, if you don't mind me saying. Why don't you spend the ten days with my wife and me I. I've been urging my wife to get to know Mrs. Kane, to see if she can persuade her to accept more help. But she's very timid and is reluctant to talk to Mrs. Kane. Perhaps you could do that?"

"Of course I could," said Mette before Frank could disagree. "Mrs. Kane sounds like someone I'd like to meet." She'd been taken by the idea that Mrs. Kane wanted to make a living for herself and her children, and was reluctant to accept charity.

Frank nodded. She could see he wasn't entirely happy with the suggestion, but it was a good way to make money in a short time.

"I can start right away," he said. "Where should I begin?"

"We know he passed through Woodville on his way to find work. That might be..."

"Woodville?" said Mette, worried suddenly. "I was in Woodville last year. Someone had recently been murdered—beaten to death in the bush."

"I wasn't going to mention it in front of you, Mrs. Hardy. But yes, there was a murder." Tomlinson wrung his hands for a minute, glancing between Frank and Mette. "And Mr. Kane passed through town at about the right time. There's been talk..."

"Right," said Frank. "That's where I'll begin. Woodville. And don't worry about me, Mette. I'm sure a murderer isn't still hanging about. I'll be quite safe."

3

To the Gorge

"Can you tell me more about this man I'm looking for?" Frank asked Tomlinson. "Age, appearance, and so on?"

Mette was in the soddy packing a bag, while the men lounged against the frame of the half-built house enjoying a smoke. Frank kept a bedroll at the ready, as he'd frequently worked away from home before he was married. It was already at his feet. All he'd had to do was stuff his saddlebags with tins from the larder, change his muddy jacket, and splash some water on his boots to clean off the mud.

"Around our age," said Tomlinson. "Mid-thirties. Irish. Dark complexion and not very tall. Five-foot six, his wife says. Thin of course. He had money with him when he left—about ninety pounds according to his wife. And he's no doubt saved more since then as he's been shearing. He was looking for land, with the idea of buying a small farm."

"Do you suspect foul play?"

"I had assumed he got himself lost in the bush," said Tomlinson. "Very easy near Woodville - the bush goes from there all the way up to Norsewood, as I'm sure you know. He was up in Waipukurau, northeast of Norsewood and would have come back on one of the bush tracks. But this thing about the murder in Woodville...well, it worries me. He had a good sum of money on him and if someone knew..."

"When was the murder, and was anyone found guilty?"

9

"November last year," said Tomlinson. "Late November. George Ollandt was the victim. Danish, like your wife. He operated a rooming house with a partner. They arrested Harry Thomsen, his mate, almost immediately, but the jury found him not guilty. Not enough evidence. Ollandt was bludgeoned to death but the coroner was sure the crime wasn't committed where the body was found. The townspeople think it was about money, and that somehow Kane - Peter Kane - got between Ollandt and Thomsen, and they fought over his money. One or the other killed him, and then Thomsen killed Ollandt, that's what they believe. It's possible."

"Does Kane's wife know about this?"

"I don't believe she does. I certainly haven't told her. She's convinced he's alive somewhere. But how he could be I have no idea. Where would he be?"

Mette came out of the soddy wearing her good dress and clutching Frank's old carpetbag. She looked excited; Frank's heart missed a couple of beats. He'd been wanting to take off and sleep rough, rather than sleep in a comfortable bed with a spring mattress, and not be spoiled by Mette's cooking. But seeing her happy about leaving gave him pause. Was she not enjoying farm life? They were so good together, she cooking and tending her garden, and he clearing the land and building their permanent house while they lived in the soddy. The nights had been good as well - better than he'd expected, other than the issue with the shift.

"Are you sure you want to go?" he asked, half hoping she'd say she'd prefer to stay with her sister and wait for him to return.

"Of course I am. I don't have as much to do as I'd like, and this will make a nice change."

"I'll put your bag in my dray, out in the lane, while you say goodbye to each other," said Tomlinson tactfully. He reached into his trouser pocket. "And here's an advance to cover your expenses." He handed Frank a bank draft. "You can cash it in at the general store in Woodville."

"I'll be off as well," said Karira. "I'll come out and check on everything every couple of days." He put his foot in the stirrup, ready to mount his horse, but stopped and turned to Frank. "And by the way, once you get the house finished I have someone who needs a place to stay and a bit of work. A young lad from the pa - Hemi his name is. He'd like to learn more about taking care of horses. He just needs a place to rest his head and three meals a day. No money, or at least not yet. He'd be a handy lad for you to have around."

"Of course," said Frank. "I'll have the house built in a month or so. He's welcome to come as soon as we've moved out of the soddy." The pa, the Maori village where Will Karira had grown up, had been sold to the government a few months earlier, and the inhabitants had been forced to leave. Frank knew it would be hard for a young Maori boy to find work in Palmerston or anywhere in the area. Frank could easily find a bit of work and food for him. A second pair of hands, even young hands, would be a welcome addition.

The two men left the yard, and Frank took Mette in his arms. "This will be the first time we've been apart since we married," he said. "Are you sure you'll be alright?"

She smiled up at him and picked off a random piece of mud that still clung to his beard. He ran his hand through his beard to brush any other dirt that had been trapped there, feeling guilty that he hadn't attempted to make himself more presentable. He'd been in too much of a hurry to take off, embracing the interesting change in his circumstances.

"I'll miss you, of course," she said. "But I can take care of myself. I hope you won't starve to death by yourself."

"Do me good," he said. "I'm getting soft." He leaned down and kissed her. "Well, goodbye then."

"Will you write?"

"If you want me to..."

"Only, I was thinking of poor Mrs. Kane. She waited such a long time without hearing from her husband. How worried she must have been."

"I'll write from Woodville," said Frank. "Or send a telegram." She was afraid he was going to disappear, he realized, like Kane. "And I'll let you know if there's anything for you to pass on to Tomlinson. But don't worry about me. I've been through the Gorge and up to Napier a hundred times when I was driving the mail coach. Nothing will happen to me."

She put her arms around his neck. "I'd die if anything did…"

"No you wouldn't," said Frank. "And neither will Mrs. Kane. He's been gone a long time. She needs to think of her children now. You concentrate on helping her and don't think about me."

She sighed. "I would die you know, but never mind." She grinned at him. "I'll go off to Sandon and have a good time. That will make you happy."

He gave her one final kiss on the forehead and stepped away from her regretfully. "Yes, it will." He almost meant it.

She left in the direction of the lane outside the farm, turning two or three times to take another look at him. He watched her, grinning, as she skipped the last few steps out of the yard. She was so young and full of joy. How had he been lucky enough to find her? Did he really want to go off on an adventure and sleep rough? He was having second thoughts…but yes, he was ready for action, for adventure. He hoped to find both. And Mette would still be there when he returned, he was sure of that.

* * *

He was forcing his way along the track towards the Gorge when he heard someone hailing him. He turned in his saddle to see who it was. A man who looked vaguely familiar was following him, spurring his horse to catch up. Frank put his hand in his coat pocket, letting it rest lightly on his gun, and squinted in the direction of the oncoming rider who had ducked to avoid overhanging branches, obscuring his face. There'd been talk of gangs of unemployed men roving in the bush, stopping riders and demanding money. Frank preferred to be cautious in this kind of situation.

"Sergeant Hardy?"

"Do I know you?"

"Dr. Johnston from Feilding. Daniel Johnston. We met last year in Palmerston, at a council meeting regarding volunteer recruitment."

"Ah, yes, of course. Are you on your way to Woodville?"

"Just to the Gorge entrance. A member of the survey party preparing the way for the train tracks injured himself...cut his foot badly with an axe. They sent a messenger to find me, but he got lost."

"Between the Gorge and Feilding? How did he manage that?"

"You know how it is. You get off the track to relieve yourself or to follow a pigeon or rabbit, and when you head back to the track you don't go quite the same way. The next thing you know..."

"I always blaze a trail," said Frank, realizing with annoyance that he'd left his Bowie knife in the soddy. "It takes very little time, and that way you can be sure..."

The doctor nodded. "Yes, well he didn't. And it took him a day to get back to the track. He was in quite a state by the time he arrived in Feilding. Rightly so...I've seen people go missing in the bush, and they're never found. Not even the bodies. Young children, sometimes, which is most disturbing..."

"I'm looking for a missing man myself," said Frank. "You've probably heard of him. Peter Kane from Sandon."

"I gave Mr. Tomlinson a donation for the widow," said the doctor. "Yes, I have heard of him."

"The widow?" said Frank. "So you think he's dead?"

"I'm sure he's dead. What else could have happened? He lost his way; he died."

They rode in silence for a time. Eventually, Johnston said, "He could have found another woman, I suppose. That happens."

"A bit hard on his wife, if that's what he's done," said Frank.

"She'll find another man to take her on," said Johnston. "There are more men in the colony than women. Even with three children, someone will see her as a good proposition. A hard worker, so I've heard, and not bad to look at."

"She probably needs to know what's happened to him before she can start thinking of remarrying. And if she's the faithful type she may not want another husband."

The doctor shrugged. "I've never met a woman who could live long without a man."

Frank occupied himself with his horse, Copenhagen, for a few minutes. It seemed the good doctor had something in his mind.

Doctor Johnston was not a man who could leave a silence empty. "Take my wife, for example," he said. "I'm sure she already has her eye on my replacement if I happen to go missing on this trip. In fact, she'd be very happy if I vanished in the bush."

"Surely not," said Frank. "You'll only be gone for a few days."

"She's awfully friendly with my partner at the surgery." The doctor gave an angry tug at the reins of his horse, to avoid a branch that hung from a tree beside the track. "She could hardly wait for me to leave...she was pulling on her hat ready for a walk into town to meet her paramour while I was fetching my horse from the paddock."

"Have you thought about divorcing her?" asked Frank. "It's been legal now for several years..."

The doctor glared at him. "Divorce? I'd be a laughing stock throughout the colony."

"But if she's the one misbehaving..."

"I'd have to prove I'd been cuckolded," said the doctor. "I'm not keen on spreading that information."

"What about letting her divorcing you?"

The doctor shook his head and dug his heels into his horse's side. "That would be worse," he said as his horse lunged forward. "She'd have to prove adultery, as well as something else - sodomy, incest, bestiality, rape, I believe are in the act—or extreme cruelty, of course. I couldn't allow her to accuse me of any of those things. I'd never work as a doctor in this country again."

On the whole, Frank thought, it sounded as if the best option for the doctor would be to disappear in the bush and appear somewhere else with another name. Easier than divorce. But what about Kane? Was his marriage in the same straits as Dr. Johnston's? Had he disappeared on purpose to get away from a difficult or unfaithful wife?

4

Mr. Harding of Sandon

Mette twisted around on the seat of the dray as Mr. Tomlinson drove away from the farm. She could see Frank still standing in the yard, hands on his hips, watching them leave. She wondered if he felt like she did, and was having second thoughts. Perhaps he was regretting that he hadn't spent any time looking for work closer to home. This morning had been the first time he'd brought up the need for work. Setting off in different directions now, so soon after they were married, felt awful. It felt permanent.

"You'll enjoy staying in Sandon," said Mr. Tomlinson suddenly. "Lots to do. Not like living out here on the land."

"I'm looking forward to it." Mette turned reluctantly away from Frank's retreating figure to pay attention to Mr. Tomlinson. "I've been to Feilding, but under different circumstances. It was..." She trailed off, remembering how Frank had been in gaol, sent there by a woman who had borne him a son many years earlier. They had crept through Feilding on the way to Wanganui, where they had gone to beard the lioness in her den. It had been a bad time for her; she had considered breaking her engagement to Frank.

"A very clean and pretty place," said Mr. Tomlinson. "Now Palmerston..."

"Palmerston is a clean and pretty town," said Mette, feeling a surge of protectiveness. "I lived there—or at least just outside town—for two years until we moved to the farm."

"You must have moved a while ago," said Tomlinson. "The smell was terrible this past summer with the heat. The council is talking about making a pit for night soil near the river. About a mile from the Square, on the Fitzherbert Street Reserve."

"That would be helpful," said Mette. She didn't really want to discuss night soil with Mr. Tomlinson and cast about for another subject. "I'd like to know more about Mrs. Kane," she said finally. "How many children does she have, and how old are they?"

"She has three," said Tomlinson. "Patrick and Thomas, the older two, are in school. And the little one—Winnie— is not much more than a baby, two or three perhaps. It's hard to tell as they're all malnourished and small for their ages."

Mette felt sad and sat back to watch the landscape as it moved slowly past, wishing she was in a buggy, speeding along with Frank, instead of plodding towards Sandon with Mr. Tomlinson in the dray. Of course Frank and Mette didn't have a buggy or a dray. If they went anywhere she would ride on Copenhagen with him. And they hardly ever went anywhere. No wonder Frank had been so happy about going off in search of Mr. Kane.

When Sandon finally came in view, she was pleasantly surprised. It was quite a large town, with a hotel, a blacksmith, and dozens of homes, as well as Mr. Tomlinson's store.

"Is there a bookshop here?" she asked.

He shook his head. "No, but I do carry some books in my store. Not novels, of course. I wouldn't carry novels. But we do have some very nice bibles and a Book of Common Prayer."

Mette looked at her hands and sighed. It was going to be quiet in Sandon. "Nothing by Mr. Dickens, perhaps?"

He shook his head firmly. "Dickens? Of course not...but if I understand you, you want something different to read. Something more entertaining?" His face showed what he thought about entertainment.

"Well, yes, if you..."

"In that case, I have Pilgrim's Progress. I haven't read it myself, but I hear it's very popular. The second most popular book in the English-speaking world. After The Bible of course."

Mette didn't know what to say about that. She'd never heard of Pilgrim's Progress, but she had a strong suspicion she wouldn't like it.

As they passed the hotel, she saw a couple come out through the main entrance, arm and arm. The woman, an attractive person with glossy dark hair beneath a pale yellow bonnet and skin the colour of alabaster, was staring up at her partner, her face full of adoration. Mette smiled and turned to Mr. Tomlinson. "Who are they? They seem to be very much in love..."

Mr. Tomlinson's lips were compressed into a tight line. "The doctor's wife." He said.

"And is that the doctor?"

"No, it is not." Mr. Tomlinson made a show of flicking his whip at the poor horse who had just dragged them all the way from the farm without complaint. She could see he did not want to discuss the couple.

He stopped waving his whip suddenly and pointed at a house, a small one in need of a good whitewash, with a front garden filled with weeds and dandelions. "Mrs. Kane's house," he said. "As you can see, it's rather run-down, but she doesn't have the time to take care of it."

As they passed the house Mette could see washing billowing in the garden behind the house. A thin woman with faded brown hair was pulling the clothes from the line, putting the pegs into her apron pouch, and dropping the freshly washed clothing into a flax basket. Mrs. Kane, she assumed. There seemed to be too much washing for such a small family. She must be taking in other people's washing, the poor woman. What a horrible way to way to make a living. She was glad she and Frank had not sunk to that level—yet.

Mr. Tomlinson cracked his whip above the horse's head once more, anxious to get home. The horse began moving at a faster pace, possibly sensing that food awaited.

A buggy driven by a man in a pale grey suit erupted from behind a tall hedge and the horse pulling the dray lurched sideways. Mr. Tomlinson wrenched it back. Mette was whipsawed one way and then another, and felt herself float up from the seat. She clutched desperately at Mr. Tomlinson's sleeve but he was too busy controlling the horse to notice what was happening to her.

She seemed to be in the air forever before she hit the road with her shoulder and tumbled towards the ditch, the gravel tearing at her arm.

"Good lord, what have I done," she heard someone say. Not Mr. Tomlinson. The voice was a rich baritone not the least like Mr. Tomlinson's scratchy nasal voice.

She sat up and brushed her sleeve. No blood, but her arm was going to ache. She was more worried about the small tears that had appeared on the left side of her skirt on her hip. She had only brought one frock with her—her good frock. Her work frock was already covered in mud from the paddock when she had helped Frank pull up the stump. She had left it at home in the wash basket, thinking she would be back in ten days and could manage that long without a change of clothing.

She had not intended to cry but felt tears seeping from the corners of her eyes. She wiped them away with the back of her hand and tried to stand up.

"Please, let me help you to your feet."

The driver of the buggy strode around the dray, his hand outstretched. Mr. Tomlinson was trying to calm the horse and keep it from tipping the dray into the ditch.

She looked up at the man who had caused the accident, ready to be angry and was met with a pair of warm blue eyes beneath a mop of fair hair.

"I hope you're not angry with me. I was in a hurry and failed to slow down as I left my house."

He held out his hands. She clasped hold of them and felt his strength as he pulled her upright.

"Oh dear," he said. He kept hold of her hands. "You're crying. Never mind. As Mr. Dickens says, it opens the lungs, washes the countenance, exercises the eyes and softens down the temper. So cry away."

Mr. Tomlinson had calmed the dray horse. He placed his whip on the seat and dropped down beside Mette...

"Mrs. Hardy, I'm so sorry. Are you hurt?"

"Mrs. Harding?" asked the stranger. "Did I get married and forget to tell myself?"

Mr. Tomlinson bobbed his head at the stranger. "I'm sorry if I almost caused an accident, Mr. Harding. This is Mrs. Hardy, not Mrs. Harding."

"Pity," said Mr. Harding. "I was quite enjoying the idea of having a wife I didn't know about. Especially such a pretty one." He let Mette's hands go finally and smiled at her.

She felt a rising tide of pink on her cheeks and bit her lip to stop it, although biting her lip had never worked before. "Did you say Dickens?" she asked. "I'm very fond of Mr. Dickens." She refrained from mentioning that she had now read A Tale of Two Cities twice, but had been unable to afford to buy any more of his books.

"As am I," he said. "I have most of his books in my library. You're free to borrow them if you'd like—are you in town long?"

"Just for ten days," she said. A library full of Mr. Dickens books, and who knew what else. Sandon had suddenly become much more interesting.

"Mrs. Hardy's husband is working for me," said Tomlinson. Mette heard him place a slight emphasis on the word husband and understood he did not approve of the way Mr. Harding had spoken to her.

"Ten days?" said Harding. "Plenty of time to finish several of Mr. Dickens' books. Will you be at the cricket match tomorrow? I'll bring one along for you."

Mette looked at Mr. Tomlinson questioningly. He nodded grudgingly. "We'll be there, of course," he said. "The match is intended to raise more funds for Mrs. Kane. I'm providing sandwiches. Some of the ladies are coming over to make them in the morning before the match starts."

"Jolly good." Harding looked at Mette again, his blue eyes holding hers. She was unable to look away. "I'll see you then. Any particular books you'd like to borrow?"

Mette's mind spun desperately. It was like being asked to choose between apple cake and rye bread cake. "David Copperfield? Bleak House?"

"I'll bring you *David Copperfield*. No one could finish Bleak House in ten days. And I have another one by Thomas Hardy you might enjoy. It's in a rural setting much like this town. Lots of sheep, if I remember correctly. And corn."

He turned to Tomlinson. "And Mr. Tomlinson. Perhaps you could join me in a pint and a pipe at the Junction Hotel after dinner tonight?"

Mr. Tomlinson muttered something that sounded like an acceptance, and Harding returned to his buggy and headed into town in a cloud of dust.

Mette climbed back onto the dray and they followed in Harding's tracks.

"Who is Mr. Harding? He doesn't seem to be the type of person you usually find in a small town like Sandon."

"Cyril Harding? He was sent here by Colonel Feilding of the Emigrants and Colonists Aid Corporation," said Tomlinson. "He's here looking for more land so the colonel can send more English settlers. He's up from Wellington for a few weeks."

"He seems very nice..."

"Why wouldn't he be?" said Tomlinson, his face sour now that Mr. Harding was out of earshot. "He's related to the Pym family through his mother. They have immense financial and political influence. He can do anything he wants, have anything he wants..." He glanced at Mette. "Stay away from him, Mrs. Hardy. He could ruin a woman like you."

Mette promised she would stay away from him, wondering at the same time what it would be like to be ruined by Mr. Harding.

5

The Accommodation House

The chief of the survey crew looked Frank up and down. "Wouldn't like a job, would you? I need someone strong who can lug the survey equipment up the slopes and isn't afraid of falling into the Gorge."

Frank eyed the group of men clustered around the survey tents. Some Scandies, the rest ex-army, by the look of them. Looked like a decent bunch of men. And he was qualified on both counts.

"What are you paying?"

"Three quid a week, all found, or if you prefer you can provide your own food and it's fifteen bob a day. We work six and a half days."

"I'm on my way through the gorge looking for a man who disappeared," said Frank. Three pounds a week wasn't much, but he could give it a few weeks if necessary. "I'll talk to you on the way back—late next week."

"We'll be here," said the crew chief. "Maybe a bit further along the Gorge. We were slowed down by the damned fool who cut his toes off. And now it's taken a day and a half for the doctor to get here."

"The man you sent got lost in the bush," said the doctor curtly. "Not my fault." He was kneeling over the injured man. "Hmm. No gangrene yet, that I can see, but I'd better snip off the rest of these toes to be on the safe side. Doesn't look like they'll be much use as they are." He rummaged in his bag. "I'll give you a whiff of chloroform before I cut."

As Frank left the camp he heard the injured man give a long, piercing scream that faded to a moan. The whiff of chloroform hadn't helped, apparently. The poor bastard would be unable to continue working with the survey team. He'd need his toes to get up the slope. Frank hoped no one was depending on his wages.

The Manawatu Gorge ran between two ranges that cut the lower part of the North Island in half. It was only five miles from one end to the other, but a treacherous five miles with frequent slips into the fast-moving torrent below. The ranges loomed on either side, flattening out towards the river. The government had built the road on the south side of the river, but the train tracks were going through on the north side. The survey team would hack out a narrow track twenty feet above the water, taking depth readings and planting pegs linked by chains to guide the men who followed. The next crew would dig out a shelf on which to build the tracks. Lucky he wasn't driving a coach anymore. There'd be no need for coaches when the train came through.

He reached the high point of the gorge and stopped to look down at the water. He'd stopped here just a few months ago, coming in the other direction, barred from going further by a tree across the road. The water still raced through a narrow channel below, and he imagined he could see the killer, still there, tumbling in the turmoil, an axe Frank had thrown at him to save Mette wedged in his head.

Frank had pulled Mette back from the brink after she had been forced over the edge by that same killer. She was terrified of heights, but she had managed to hold on long enough for him to lower himself down holding the reins of one of his horses and pull her up. She was shivering with fright and he had held her close, vowing to himself to protect her forever.

At the spot where the ambush had been set, the hill had started to crumble. The loss of the tree had loosened the soil, and a small spray of stones and dirt splayed out to the middle of the road. He got down to check. The soil was moist. Any more rain and there'd be a full slide. He remounted Copenhagen and spurred her towards Woodville. Better let them know.

It was dusk as he reached the town and a steady rain was falling. He'd need to find a place to stay soon. A candle flickered in the window of Murphy's Hotel. He pounded on the door and Mr. Murphy opened it instantly. He was wearing a striped nightshirt and holding a candle.

"I'm just on the way to bed. Ah—Sergeant Hardy. What brings you here? I heard you weren't driving the mail coach anymore."

"No, I've gone into horse farming. Do you have a room for the night?"

Mr. Murphy shook his head. "Sorry. I have a group from up north going through the Gorge tomorrow on a tour...but I'll have a bed tomorrow night. How long do you intend to stay?"

"I'm not sure," said Frank. He stepped back and looked down the street. "Are there any other places in town I could find a bed? I'll need stabling for my horse as well..."

"You can leave your horse in my stable," said Murphy. "If you have a blanket with you, you could kip in the accommodation house across the way. It's closed, but I've seen a few swagmen sneaking in there. Still got some beds. You'd be comfortable enough if you're used to sleeping rough. Keep an eye open for swagmen coming in though. They're mostly harmless, but there've been one or two who've tried to jump people going through the bush. Desperation, mostly."

"Are the owners around anywhere?"

"Not exactly." Mr. Murphy looked as if he was about to confide something but decided not to. "One's dead and the other one...he left town. The insurance company owns...."

A querulous voice called out from a back room, and Mr. Murphy spun around. "I'll be there in a moment, dear."

Frank warned him of the potential for a slip in the Gorge and took his horse around to the livery stable. Across the road at the accommodation house, a hand-painted sign on the door, apparently put there by the insurance agents, admonished him that trespassing was forbidden. The wooden front door was rickety and creaked loudly as he pushed it open.

"Anyone here?"

Quiet, other than the sound of rain drumming on the corrugated iron roof.

To the right of the door, what seemed to have once been a bakery stood empty. He walked down a hallway with rooms on either side and picked the last one, which at least had a window. To say it had a bed was an exaggeration. A bench with a thin, lumpy straw mattress and no blankets took up most of the room. He picked up the mattress and flipped it over, shaking it, to make sure there were no bed bugs or other vermin living inside. It looked somewhat clean, although there was a smear of what could be dried blood across the area where the pillow would rest. He turned it back the way he had found it, threw down his bedroll and stretched out. His feet hung over the end of the bed, but it wasn't the worst accommodation he'd been in. He chewed on a piece of bread slathered with sardines and thought about what he was going to do next. He'd have to talk to townspeople, starting with Mr. Murphy at the hotel.

He wished Mette was with him and wondered briefly why he hadn't suggested she come along. It wasn't as if Woodville was a dangerous town. No more dangerous than Palmerston or Sandon. He thought about the tour group staying in Murphy's Hotel, obviously not worried about travelling in the district. They would be couples and families, he was sure, and none of them would have seen the kinds of danger Mette had faced. Eventually, he drifted off, the low drumbeat of the rain soothing him.

Something awoke him. The rusty hinges of the front door creaked as someone closed it. He grabbed his gun from under the pillow and slid off the bed towards a dark corner where he would be hard to see. He heard footsteps in the hallway, hesitant, shuffling, as if the person was unsure of himself. Then the door to his room opened slowly.

Someone stood there, silhouetted by moonlight from the window. Frank gave him a minute, then said quietly, "Looking for someone?"

The man jumped. "What the...who are you? What are you doing in his bedroom?"

Frank had his gun out, held loosely in one hand. "Whose bedroom?"

The man lurched forward and sat down heavily on the bed. "George's bedroom, of course. He was the owner. Don't you know...?"

"The owner who left town?"

The man wiped his eyes as if he had been crying. "Of course not. He's dead. He was murdered. Don't you know about him?"

"George Ollandt lived in this house?"

The man took a few minutes to compose himself, nodding all the while. "He was...he was...the owner."

"And he was a friend of yours?"

When the man did not reply, Frank asked, "And what about the man who was accused of murdering him?"

"That was Harry Thomsen," said the man. "Harry lived here too, but it was really George's place. Harry just took advantage of him. He sat down heavily on the bed. "Harry was younger, and George was blind to what he was really like. Poor George."

Frank thought he was getting the picture. He'd spent twenty years in the British Army, after all. "And George was a...friend of yours? I mean, before Harry turned up?"

The man nodded. "George went up to Napier for the day and came back with Harry. After that, he had no time for me. Harry was exciting. Everyone liked him. He told stories about his time in Australia—bushrangers and black-fellows, stuff like that. And he liked to gamble, especially with George's money."

Frank slid his gun into his trouser pocket and leaned against the window sill. "Did you ever come across a man named Peter Kane? He passed through Woodville a year ago, and he may have been here at the time of the murder of George Ollandt."

"So they say."

"So who says?"

The man shrugged. "Everyone says. They think Harry murdered him. I wouldn't be surprised."

"Did you see Mr. Kane here at the time of the murder?"

"I don't remember. It was such a shock, you see, finding George like that, all bloodied. I couldn't think of anything..."

"And you believe it was Harry who did it? Killed George?"

"Of course it was. Who else would it be? He said he hated George, right before George was killed. Everyone heard him. And he said he saw the body when he couldn't have. How did he know where George's body was?"

Frank thought for a while and said finally, "Why would people say Harry killed Peter Kane? Do they give a reason? Was he...one of your type?"

The man lay back on the bed abruptly. "I don't want to talk about it anymore. I'm going to go to sleep on his bed now. You can find somewhere else to sleep."

Frank pulled his bedroll off the bed, picked up his clothes and retreated to another room. He had a lot more questions, including the name of his new acquaintance, but they could wait until morning.

6

Meeting her Match

"Good morning Mrs. Hardy. I have the book I promised you."

Mette was sitting in the garden of the Tomlinson house enjoying the late spring sunshine. She knew it would make her face red, but she didn't care; she disliked the appearance of pale skin that most women craved. Mr. Tomlinson's copy of Pilgrim's Progress lay across her lap, opened at the first page. She was pretending Frank was nearby in another chair, but feeling somewhat out of sorts because he was not.

She opened her eyes and saw Mr. Harding smiling down at her, his fair curls, lit from behind, surrounding his head like a halo. She sat up, excited. "Is it one of Mr. Dickens…?"

"Unfortunately not. I thought I had some copies of Dickens in my library, but I was mistaken. But this one looks…is very good."

Mette took the book, trying to hide her disappointment.

"*Paul Clifford*, by Bulwer Litton," she said, turning it over. I've never heard of Mr. Litton. Have you read it?"

"Several times," he said. "It's set during the French Revolution. The hero is a gentleman who leads a double life as a highwayman. He's arrested and taken before a judge, who, unbeknownst to him, is his own father…"

That sounded a little close to home for Mette. She took the book and read the first line aloud. "It was a dark and stormy night…" She smiled up at Mr. Harding. "A good opening line at least. Thank you very much."

He looked relieved, although she had no idea why.

"Are you going to the cricket match this afternoon?" he asked.

She nodded. "I spent all morning with the local ladies making sandwiches. I was resting before tackling the next thing, which is arranging some of Mr. Tomlinson's garden chairs beside the cricket pitch for people who prefer not to sit on the grass. Will you be there?"

"Yes. The captain of the club asked me to play just this morning. They're short a player at deep midwicket, Dr. Johnston's position. I'd prefer wicketkeeper, but the captain normally plays in that position. I was happy to fill in wherever they needed me. Their loss, of course."

"My husband enjoys cricket," said Mette. She wasn't used to people being so confident about their own skills. Frank would never boast like that. "He used to play with the sons of his father's employer when they were home from school."

"What school was that?" he asked.

"Rugby," said Mette. "I always think it's odd for a school to be named for a game. But it's a good school, apparently. Where did you go to school?"

"Eton," he said.

"So you're an old boy of Eton." Mette had learned about Old Boys from the Rev. Masterson, the Chaplain of Wanganui Collegiate, who'd officiated at her wedding.

"An Old Etonian, more correctly," he said, smiling. "Well, I'd best be away. I shall see you this afternoon."

Mette sat back and let the sun bathe her face again. She felt content. One day in Sandon, and already she'd met someone else who liked books, and several townswomen who had treated her like an old friend. Mr. Tomlinson was such a nice man. Mrs. Tomlinson, who was a good bit younger than her husband, seemed to be a pleasant person as well, judging by her looks, although Mette had not heard her say anything since she'd arrived the previous night, other than "Yes, dear" or "Of course, dear." No wonder Mr. Tomlinson needed someone to speak with Mrs. Kane. They'd sat through the evening meal exchanging smiles in near silence.

The women of Sandon had gossiped about Mrs. Kane while they spread sardines and potted chicken with sliced cucumbers for the sandwiches. One woman had brought two large pound cakes with her and complained that she hadn't been able to leave the cakes to cool on the window sill as she was afraid one of the Kane boys would steal them. She'd seen Patrick Kane hanging around outside the kitchen window.

"Probably starving, the poor thing," said Mrs. Johnston. "You should have cut him a piece of cake to take home." Mrs. Johnston was the doctor's wife, the very same woman Mette had seen coming out of the Albion Hotel the previous day, clinging lovingly to a man who was not Dr. Johnston.

"With all the help we're giving her, you'd think his mother would manage to buy the children something to eat," said the pound-cake baker.

"I believe she's refused to take any of the money Mr. Tomlinson collected," said Mrs. Johnston. "So foolish of her."

"How does she manage, without money?" Mette asked.

"She lives rent-free, thanks to Mr. Tomlinson," said Mrs. Johnston. "And she works at the Albion Hotel every morning, making up the rooms from the previous night. It's very little pay, of course —sixpence a room — and sometimes only one or two rooms are used so she goes home with a shilling. The publican lets her take kitchen scraps from the breakfast table. They pretend it's for her animals, even though we all know she doesn't have any animals."

"I saw her hanging out washing yesterday," said Mette. "Too much washing for one family. Do you think she's taking some in?"

Mrs. Johnston shrugged, but from the look on her face, Mette guessed she was giving her washing to Mrs. Kane, and not paying her much for her labour.

The cricket match started as soon as everyone had their fill of sandwiches and pound cake. Mette found a place on the grass not far from where Mr. Harding stood. Mr. Harding was wearing a white jersey and white boots and looked very dashing. Mr. Moore, Mrs. Johnston's friend from the hotel, was also playing deep midwicket and stood beside Mr. Harding. Mrs. Johnston, resplendent in pale grey and mauve, with a stylish pale grey straw hat she had obviously not purchased in Sandon, sat down next to Mette on the grass.

"A fine-looking pair," she said, smiling fondly towards the men, who were chatting like old friends.

"I met Mr. Harding for the first time yesterday," said Mette, feeling the need to correct any false impressions Mrs. Johnston might have of her relationship to Mr. Harding.

"Lucky for you he's not spoken for yet," said Mrs. Johnston. "I think he's quite taken with you...he was saying..."

"I'm married," said Mette. "And quite recently. I met Frank—my husband—six months ago, and we married before Christmas."

"Too soon, I suppose," said Mrs. Johnston enigmatically.

They watched the match in silence. Mette had no idea what was happening, but she enjoyed sitting in the fresh air. She wondered if Frank would like to live in a town like this. He enjoyed male company and was good at sports, especially games where he could use his size to advantage.

She heard a disturbance over near the picnic tables. Turning, she saw an older man holding a small, freckled boy by the ear. The boy had stuffed his mouth full of sandwiches and was grabbing handfuls of cake even as he was pulled away.

"Patrick Kane," said Mrs. Johnston. "I don't know why he shouldn't eat some of the sandwiches. We're raising money for his mother to buy food, after all."

Mr. Tomlinson hurried over to intervene, and the boy was allowed to finish eating. She would visit Mrs. Kane the next day, Mette decided, and find out what she would be willing to accept from the townspeople. Surely she didn't want her children to starve.

Mr. Harding did not have to do much. He stood at his position, leaning forward, slapping his fist into his gloved palm, ready to catch any balls that came his way, while offering his opinion to the rest of his team about what they should be doing. Mette began to realize that being ruined by Mr. Harding would not be as exciting as she had first thought. Not that she had given it any real consideration—she had her wonderful Frank, after all. It was just the thought of all those books...

After what seemed like hours, a whack presaged the flight of a ball in Mr. Harding's direction. The crowd roared, but Mr. Harding had chosen that exact moment to scratch his ankle.

"Harding, Harding..."

Mr. Harding straightened, but it was too late. The ball was almost on him. Everyone held their collective breath.

From the sidelines, Patrick Kane, running at full speed, ran out onto the field. At the last minute, he threw himself forward and caught the ball seconds before it hit the ground. The crowd roared and whistled.

The umpire blew his whistle and waved the catch away.

"He's not a member of the team. Doesn't count," he called.

"Of course it does," protested Harding. He took hold of Patrick Kane's wrist and held his hand aloft. "He caught the ball just as I was about to. I would certainly have caught it."

But the umpire shook his head and the game continued.

After the other team had run up and down between the wickets for an hour or so more, tapping their bats on the ground as they reached the ends, everyone changed places. Mr. Harding's team was now at bat, and the other team was in the field.

"Is the game nearly over?" she asked Mrs. Johnston.

"Halfway," said Mrs. Johnston. "You're lucky. Sometimes they play for days. And they never stop talking about it. My husband adores cricket. We went down to Wellington to see the touring English Cricket Team last year, and he was devastated when two of their members were arrested for malicious injury of property."

"I thought cricket players were gentlemen," said Mette.

"You'd think so," said Mrs. Johnston. She fanned her face with her shawl to cool herself. "But a man's true character comes out when he plays cricket."

Finally, the match ended. Mette stood and stretched. Mr. Harding, who had scored several runs during his team's innings, came over, smiling proudly. "Well Mrs. Hardy? Did you enjoy yourself?"

She smiled politely. "Yes, of course."

"Now when you've finished the book...the...um..."

"Paul Clifford?"

"Yes, of course. The book by Paul Clifford. When you've finished that book, you'll have to see my library and choose the next book for yourself."

She had decided she did not like Mr. Harding, who could not remember the name of the author of the book he claimed to have read several times. But once more she was tempted by the thought of all those books. "I'd love to see your library," she said.

7

The Woodville Murder

Frank woke the next day feeling old. His mouth was dry and he was hungry enough to eat a horse. He'd eaten horse meat once; it was edible, although tough. But that was during a forced march. Now he fancied a good egg breakfast with bread and butter. He'd thought he could still live rough, but it wasn't starting well.

The man he'd left sleeping on the murder victim's bed was gone, leaving no sign that he'd been there. Frank took his bedroll and left, hoping Murphy would find him a bed that night.

Outside it was raining steadily, and he hopped between puddles to Murphy's hotel across the road. He was met with the smell of bacon frying and the sound of voices of people chattering excitedly. The tour group was gathering in the dining room.

"Good morning Sergeant. Sleep well?" Murphy was fussing around the tour group, pouring large cups of tea and doling out fried bread, eggs, and pork sausage breakfasts as they came from the kitchen.

Frank's mouth watered as he watched the steaming breakfast plates move past him. Exactly what he felt like. He'd become accustomed to Mette's *morgenmad*, which usually consisted of liver paste or herrings followed by bread and jam. The return to a good English breakfast would be welcome. "Well enough. But I'm hoping you'll have a room available for tonight if I decide to stay."

Murphy tilted his head towards the tour group, a dozen men and women dressed in their best clothes, their faces alight with excitement about the day before them. "They're going through the Gorge, even in this rain. I'll certainly have a bed for you."

"I saw the potential for a slip when I came through the Gorge yesterday," said Frank. "The land looked very unstable. Tell the coachman to keep an eye open."

"I can tell him," said Murphy. "But they won't be stopped from going. They've come all the way from Napier and have a hotel booked in Palmerston tonight. They're ready for an adventure. I just hope they don't get more than they're bargaining for."

Frank sat and waited until a plate of food arrived in front of him. As he started to eat, Mr. Murphy sat down opposite him and slid a key across the table. "You can have a room at the back of the hotel. Number Ten to the left at the top of the stairs. The bed accommodates only one person, so I hope you're not anticipating company."

"I'm a married man," said Frank, taking the key. "I'm sure the bed will do very well."

Mr. Murphy shrugged. "As you wish. But you didn't tell me yesterday why you're here. Why would you want to stay in Woodville for more than a night?"

Frank put down his knife and fork. "I'm looking for someone. Someone who left Sandon almost a year ago and has disappeared. He went through Woodville last June and his wife heard from him in November saying he was on the way home. Then nothing."

"Peter Kane," said Murphy. "I was wondering when someone was going to come looking for him."

"You remember him?"

"I never saw him," said the hotel owner. "But others have said he was here on the way from Sandon. And we heard he was heading back this way around the time of the murder. Townspeople generally think he must have been involved somehow. The timing is right. Maybe he came out of the Forty Mile Bush on the far side of town and ran into the murder as it happened."

"I met a man in the accommodation house last night," said Frank. "He didn't tell me his name, but he said he was sure Harry Thomsen was guilty because he saw the body. I wasn't sure what he meant by that."

Mr. Murphy steepled his fingers and looked at the tabletop. "Samuel Kemp," he said. "I've seen him going in there late at night. He was there when we found the body, and...well let me start from the beginning." He cleared his throat. "Tom Fountaine, the storekeeper, and Harry Thomsen came to the hotel at eight in the morning on the 23rd of November and told me George was missing. They were going to look for him. He'd been out in the bush splitting palings the previous evening and hadn't returned. I said I'd join them and we went out, with a few more chaps from town, and found the stump where he'd been splitting his palings. His tools were there, and his maul, with the handle shorn off. We thought he might have gone off to cut himself another handle. Maybe he'd hurt himself and was bleeding badly somewhere. We followed in the direction we thought he might have gone, and found a tree partially cut down. Harry claimed he could see tracks, and he led us off into the bush. I couldn't see anything, but he said he knew George's boot print."

"He knew where he was going, then," said Frank. "That's what Kemp meant when he said Harry knew where the body was?"

"More than that," said Murphy. "But I'll get to that. We searched for two, two and a half hours, mostly following Harry's lead. Eventually, someone called out, 'What a horrible sight'—or 'plight'—I'm not sure which. But Samuel was nearer to Harry and he said that it was Harry who said it, and that Harry was not near enough to the body to see that it was a horrible sight. Or even to see the body itself. That's what got Harry arrested, really. Samuel going on about him not being able to see the body. Of course, Samuel's sorry he said it now. He feels guilty, even though Harry got off."

"And there was no suggestion, at this point, that Peter Kane was in the area? No one mentioned his name or said they'd seen him?"

"Not at that time. It was just when we heard he'd gone missing that we started to put two and two together."

"Is it possible Peter Kane was the murderer? Harry Thomsen was acquitted, you said?"

Murphy pulled at his lower lip, thinking. "No," he said finally. "It's possible I suppose. But no one really believes Harry is innocent. There was other evidence—the body had been moved; there was blood on the pillow in George's bedroom; he'd been fighting with George. But the judge found there wasn't a chain of evidence. Where was he killed? How did the body get to where it was? Harry couldn't have killed him in the bedroom and then carried him out to where we found him. George was too heavy, and someone would certainly have seen him."

"What about Kemp?" asked Frank. "Could he have helped Harry? Carried the body out, for example?"

Murphy shook his head. "Kemp was in the bar at my hotel all day on the 22nd. He would have had to do everything at night, including murdering George and carrying the body into the bush. And you know how dark it gets at night around here."

Frank finished his breakfast and put the room key in his pocket. "Thanks for breakfast. And for the information. I have to cash in a bank draft. I'll be back later to pay for everything."

"Tom Fountaine at the general store will cash a bank draft," said Murphy. "And you can talk to him about the murder. He had a better look at the whole thing than I did. Finding the body, I mean. And he sees most people who pass through town. Maybe he saw Peter Kane and can help you somehow."

Frank took his bank draft to the store and found Tom Fountaine, a man in his mid-thirties with a trim moustache and receding hair, seated behind the counter, organizing what looked like a pile of bills. Without looking up, Fontaine asked, "Can I assist you with something?"

"I have a bank draft I'd like to cash. Ten pounds. Could you manage that?"

Fontaine sighed heavily and pushed the papers aside. "I suppose I can. It'll clean me out, but the agent for the Bank of New Zealand will be through in a few days." He pulled open a drawer and withdrew ten one-pound notes. "Haven't I seen you in Woodville before? You look familiar."

"I used to come through in my coach—I drove the Royal Mail coach for a year or two."

"Ah, of course. And what brings you to Woodville now?"

"I'm looking for a missing man, name of Peter Kane. An acquaintance of his wife hired me to see if I can find out what happened to him. We believe he's dead, of course, but his wife would like to be more certain. Did you see him when he went through Woodville?"

Fontaine nodded. "Of course. I see everyone who passes through here. They buy supplies from me. I didn't see him coming back, but you heard about the murder I suppose?"

"I've heard of nothing but the murder," said Frank. "The whole town seems to think Peter Kane got mixed up in it somehow, but nobody knows how or why."

Fontaine leaned towards Frank and tapped on the counter. "Two questions," he said. "Murder is usually for love or money. So then. Was Kane carrying any money? Was another woman involved? Or a man? He could have been 'that way'. Other people in this town are."

"He is—was—a married man with three children, so as far as I know he wasn't 'that way.'" Frank thought for a minute, remembering the brutal floggings he'd seen in his time in the army for men who were 'that way.' "Why do you suggest he might be?"

"Well, I wondered about George Ollandt and Harry Thomsen, to be honest. Ollandt was older, and he met Thomsen up in Napier and more or less made him his partner. But they used to fight like an old married couple."

"I met a man last night, Samuel Kemp, who broke into the accommodation house and wanted to sleep in Ollandt's bed," said Frank. "I was sleeping there because Mr. Murphy didn't have a room for me. Kemp was determined that I had to move and let him have the bed. He said it was 'his bed', meaning George Ollandt's bed, I presume."

"That explains a few things," said Fontaine. "His word almost convicted Thomsen in the trial. If we'd know he was jealous his word wouldn't have carried as much impact. As it was Harry was found not guilty, so no harm was done."

"You think Kemp lied? Weren't you with him when you found the body?"

"I was, and I was a witness at the trial as well."

"What did you see when you neared the body?"

"Well, we'd been searching for more than two hours. Eleven o'clock it was. I heard someone say, "Here's a terrible sight." I went towards the caller and found Samuel Kemp standing beside Harry Thomsen, about sixty feet from the body. Kemp said, 'Harry says he can see the body.' We all moved closer, and then we saw it— the body." He rubbed his eyes and continued. "It was a terrible sight, as Harry had said. George's face was cut in two, one eye was gone and his nose was partly cut away. He'd been hit with a bill hook, which he would have carried with him to cut a new handle for his maul, although there was no sign of the weapon itself."

"A crime of passion, by the sound of it," said Frank.

"There was definitely a lot of passion involved. Hate, very strong hate. The wounds were terrible. Ollandt had a dice box on his breast for some reason. Maybe it was something to do with Harry gambling. George used to complain about that. And there was a candle nearby. Harry lifted up the body—he seemed very calm I thought—and we found a box of matches and a page torn from a religious magazine underneath him, both spotted with blood. The police found the rest of the magazine in George's room later that day. Harry put his hand in George's pocket and took out a purse and opened it. Looking to see if George had been robbed, I suppose. The thing was, there was no indication that George had been killed on that spot. No signs of a struggle, and not much blood considering the wounds. Harry was arrested the next day, partly because of the blood on the pillow, and the page torn from the magazine, but also, as I said, because Samuel Kemp insisted that he'd said he'd seen the body when he couldn't have. Harry was tried and found not guilty. The paper said 'Not Proven' would be more appropriate."

"I have to ask again," said Frank. "In all this, no reason to think that Peter Kane was involved, or even in town."

"Not really. Although there was one thing that seemed strange."

"What was that?" asked Frank.

"I heard he—Kane—sold his horse to Mr. Monteith, my partner. Why would he do that? He had a long walk ahead of him, looking for work. You'd think he'd need his horse."

"That was on his way through Woodville the first time, wasn't it?" asked Frank. "I'll talk to Monteith. He may know something."

* * *

Frank tracked down Mr. Monteith at his home. Henry Monteith was a short, broad-chested Scot with the upright posture of a man who was confident of his position in the world. Although he was in his fifties, he still had a full head of red hair, swept back from his forehead in a wave.

"I heard Peter Kane sold you his horse, and I wondered if you could tell me anything about him. What he said to you, why he felt the need to sell the horse..."

Monteith sighed and rubbed his eyes. "It's very hard to be changing a story, once people have it in their heads," he said. "I tell people over and over again—and the police know about this—that it wasn't me who bought yon Peter Kane's horse."

"It wasn't? Then who...?"

"My son," said Monteith. "He's also Henry."

"Could I speak with your son?" asked Frank. "Where would I find him?"

Monteith gestured vaguely eastward. "He's up in Waipukurau," he said. "Fifty miles northeast of here, through the Forty Mile Bush. He's a land agent up there."

"When did this happen, the sale, do you know?"

Monteith shook his head. "Not at all. The police went up to see him last month, but he was away. He was wed in March and took his new wife to Australia for a holiday—a honeymoon. I'm thinking they'll be back now."

Frank thought for a minute. "Waipukurau is not far from Waipawa, where Kane supposedly deposited twenty pounds in the bank."

"I hadn't heard about that," said Monteith. "They're close, the two towns. A healthy man could walk from one town to the next in an hour. And twenty pounds is around what my son would have paid for the horse, so Kane could have put the money from the sale in the bank. And there isn't a bank in Waipukurau, so he'd need to go to Waipawa to deposit his money."

"Why would he not put all his money in the bank? Apparently, he already had ninety pounds when he left home, and he'd been working."

"He came into my store on his way through Woodville and purchased a lockbox from me," said Monteith. "I did wonder why he'd need a lockbox—if someone robbed him they'd just take it and smash it open."

"Do you think he could have intended to hide the money somewhere?" said Frank. "He knew it was dangerous carrying all that money through the Forty Mile Bush. He would have planned to get it on the way home. If that was the case, where would he hide it?"

"That's the question," said Monteith. "You'll have fifty miles to search if you want to find that out. Mebbe he said something to my son?"

Frank left Mr. Monteith feeling no closer to an answer. If Kane had hidden his lockbox somewhere near Woodville and had gone to collect it on the way home, perhaps either Ollandt or Thomsen had come across him and the meeting had led to two murders. He needed to talk to Mr. Monteith's son.

He returned to the hotel to let Mr. Murphy know he was leaving Woodville and would not be needing a bed that night. As he was saddling up Copenhagen, Samuel Kemp, his companion from the previous night at the accommodation house, came lurching down the street. He was clutching a half-empty gin bottle to his chest, his hair wild, his face grey and drawn.

"Hey, you," he said putting his hand on Copenhagen's saddle and staring up at Frank with bleary eyes. "You were there last night, weren't you? In his bed."

Frank nodded. "I'm leaving town, Kemp. You'll have the house to yourself tonight."

"Before you go..." Kemp stopped and wiped his nose on his sleeve. "Before you go, I want to talk to you. I have terrible ideas in my head...I can't tolerate them anymore...I need to talk to someone."

"Is it something to do with Peter Kane?"

"Who the hell is...? No, I want to talk to you about Harry...Harry Thomsen. And about George. And the others..."

"I don't have time now," said Frank. "I have to get moving before the sun goes down. I can't ride through the bush in the dark."

"That's the thing," said Kemp. "The bush. I wanted to tell you about what we did in the bush. You'd understand. You were a soldier..."

Frank hoisted himself up onto Copenhagen. "Sorry. I don't have time. I'll be back in a day or two. Talk to me then."

Kemp tottered away. "I'll tell someone else..." he said. "It's bad, what we did...the lie..."

For a minute, Frank considered dismounting and hearing Kemp out. But he was being paid to find out what had happened to Peter Kane, not to get involved in the sordid goings-on in Woodville. And he had to get to Waipukurau. He couldn't take the time to listen to Kemp's ramblings. They would keep until he got back. By then he would know more about what had happened to Peter Kane.

8

Mary Kane

Mette felt nervous when she knocked on Mary Kane's door the next morning. She was carrying a flax basket filled with the leftover sandwiches from the previous day—the pound cakes had both been eaten—and the money raised from the cricket match and the picnic was tucked in her skirt pocket: two pounds, one shilling and sixpence, all in coins. But she was worried that Mary Kane would spurn both offerings and had no idea what she was going to say to change her mind.

She had practiced her greeting, but as the door opened and Mary Kane stood there frowning, wiping her hands on her apron, her whole mien unfriendly and unwelcoming, Mette's mind went blank. "Good morning Mrs. Kane, "I'm Mette Jensen, and I...I'm sorry...I'm Mette Hardy and..."

Mary Kane looked her up and down and said sharply, "I don't think I know you, do I? What are you after, then?"

"I'm staying with Mr. Tomlinson while my husband searches for your husband. He used to work as an investigator and Mr. Tomlinson..."

"Mr. Tomlinson hired an investigator to find Peter? He never said a thing about that to me."

"He wanted to give you peace of mind."

"He wanted to spend the money he'd collected for me, more like. He knew I wouldn't take it. Is your husband a friend of Mr. Tomlinson?"

Mette heard the emphasis Mary Kane placed on the word friend, which hinted that Mr. Tomlinson might be redirecting the money to someone he knew. "No, he isn't a friend...my husband was a soldier, a sergeant in the army," she said defensively. "And then for a while he had his own investigative agency in Palmerston, with a partner. Now we have a horse farm. But his partner brought Mr. Tomlinson out to the farm because..."

"The British Army?" asked Mary Kane, her lips tightening into a thin line.

"He's a very good man," said Mette. "I wouldn't have married him otherwise."

Mary Kane's eyes narrowed. "You married him because he was a good man?"

Mette asked tentatively, "May I come in?"

Mary Kane stepped back and waved Mette inside. "I don't have a place to sit, but you can come in and stand. I don't suppose you live in a palace yourself. You're a Scandi, aren't you? Married to a British soldier. Very strange."

The house was tiny, just one room with no furniture, not even a bed. There was no sign of food, and she wondered what Mr. Kane cooked with, or how the family ate. A small fireplace with a blackened pot looked as if it hadn't been used for a while, and there were no plates or cutlery in evidence. In the corner, a small girl lay on the floor on a pile of clothes, her thumb in her mouth. She took out her thumb and said, "Mama? Taties?"

"This is my youngest," said Mary Kane. "She was christened Mary Winifred, the same as me. But we always call her Winnie. Come here darlin'"

Winnie tottered towards her mother and clung to her skirts. She looked sideways at Mette, her thumb back in her mouth.

"What a pretty child," said Mette. She opened her basket and pulled out one of the sardine and cucumber sandwiches. "Is it all right if I give her one of these?" Mary Kane nodded. Mette passed the sandwich to Winnie Kane, who took it eagerly and began chewing on the crust.

"I saw your eldest boy—Patrick, is it? —at the picnic yesterday. He ran out and caught a ball. He threw himself forward and landed on his stomach, and still managed to catch it. I was very impressed. But it didn't count as he isn't on the team."

Mary Kane actually let herself smile, her lips curving upwards. Mette could see the resemblance to her daughter. She was thinner, of course, but with large blue eyes beneath a high forehead. Her light brown hair had streaks of grey, but still retained a hint of auburn.

"He'd love to join the team," she said. "But they won't have him."

"Is he too young?" asked Mette.

"So they say," said Mrs. Kane. "But I think they don't want an Irish child playing with them. Mr. Metard's son, James, is on the team, and he's just a year older."

"Mrs. Kane—Mary."

"Yes?"

Mette took the coins from her pocket. "We collected this at the cricket match yesterday. It's only two pounds or so, but because your son was playing—in a way he was playing—perhaps you wouldn't mind taking it. Mr. Tomlinson put out a billy can and everyone threw in change. They're very worried about you, about how you're managing."

Mary Kane scooped the change from Mette's outstretched hand. "Thank Mr. Tomlinson," she said. "And tell him I don't want any more. I can manage perfectly well. And my brother's sending me some money from Palo Alto—that's in California."

"Shall I leave the sandwiches somewhere?"

"Put them on the floor where Winnie was sleeping. The boys will have them when they get home from school. Would you like to go outside? It's stuffy in here."

A clothesline stretching across the yard billowed with freshly washed sheets. Mary Kane set Winnie on her hip and moved along the row pressing each sheet against her face to see if any of them were dry. "Nearly done," she said. "Would you like to sit on the tree branch for a time? You can tell me how a nice Scandi woman like you came to be married to a British soldier."

They sat on a dip in a low-hanging branch of an aged willow tree. The tree made Mette feel calmer. She hadn't realized how jittery she'd been feeling, and how much Frank's presence relaxed her and made her feel safe. "Frank and I were married two months ago," she said. "We met last year when he offered to search for my cousin and a friend who had disappeared. We just...I can't explain it, but we just seemed perfect for each other."

Mary Kane hugged her daughter and smiled. "I understand you exactly. Peter and I met in Hokitika and we married very quickly as well. I was a housemaid to a woman named Mrs. O'Grady. Peter was a miner up at the Blue Spur. Trying to be at least."

"Hokitika?" asked Mette. "Where's that?"

"Down in the South Island, on the West Coast. It's a gold mining town. Very rough. The Burgess Gang went through that year—they killed a surveyor before they killed all those poor miners up near Nelson."

"How scary. Was it safe for a woman, with all those gold miners?"

"I can handle difficult men," said Mary. "And Mrs. O'Grady was a very strong woman. She kept the cash for all the men in her safe. All the Irish men, I mean. They trusted her."

"You and your husband were...are...both Irish then?"

Mary Kane ignored Mette's slip of the tongue. "That was what brought us together. Not just that we were both Irish, but that the Irish were so looked down on and we felt it was us against the world. The Fenians rioted in Hokitika earlier that year—a man was killed. They were causing trouble all around the world: inciting soldiers at Aldershot, invading Canada, rioting in Boston. So people weren't very keen on the Irish, even though we aren't all Fenians. Peter and I, we just wanted to be together from the moment we met."

"That was how I felt, as well," said Mette.

Mary Kane turned and looked at Mette critically. "Was he your first? Your husband I mean."

"My first?" Mette felt a rising tide of pink creeping up her neck from her chest. "You mean...?" She had agonized over whether or not she should give herself to Frank before they married, egged on by her sister Maren who had arrived in New Zealand already pregnant, and had married her shipboard paramour as soon as she arrived. But Mette had waited, well, waited at least until the night before the wedding. Then it was all so pleasant she'd wondered why she had bothered.

"I suppose he was then," said Mary Kane. "Peter was the same. The only man I ever slept with. And now I miss him so much. I'd give anything to have him in my bed again."

Mette hesitated, wondering how much she could ask. "Did you wait until you were married?"

Mary Kane nodded firmly. "Of course we did. You couldn't go and get yourself pregnant if you wanted to keep your job." Mette saw a small smile flit across her face. Mary Kane was staring back down at the past, remembering something. She rubbed her palm on her skirt. "But there were other things…"

Mette had not yet been daring enough to sleep with Frank without her shift on. She didn't want any more details about how Mary and Peter Kane had satiated themselves before they were married. She changed the subject quickly. "It must have been difficult, all of you in one room."

Mary Kane laughed. "I listened to my parents, and my children listened to us. That's the way things are when you're poor. When you're young it doesn't bother you." She hugged her daughter. "You don't know what's happening, do you, Winnie? You think all that groaning is your father snoring or having a nightmare, and then as you get older and understand what they're doing, you cover your ears and hope it won't last too long. By then it usually doesn't."

The first thing she was going to do back at the farm, Mette decided, was build the new house and get out of the one-roomed soddy. One of these days she'd be pregnant, and the thought of doing what she and Frank did with a child in the room filled her with dismay.

She left Mary Kane, her emotions in a turmoil. She had to admit to herself that she was missing Frank physically. And they never had any problems finding things to talk about. It was just that she had been hoping to find someone with whom she could discuss books and music.

As if by magic, Cyril Harding appeared from the gateway of his house. "Good morning Mrs. Hardy," he said. "You look somewhat flustered. Is there something I can do to assist you?"

She shook her head, avoiding his eyes. "I was visiting Mary Kane," she said. "I took her some sandwiches from the picnic yesterday. Her husband is missing—as I'm sure you know—and she's very poor. Mr. Tomlinson has very kindly been collecting money for her, but she's refused to take it."

He stared down the street towards Mary Kane's house. "Yes…I offered my assistance as well, but she wouldn't take anything from me either."

"That was very kind," said Mette. Mr. Harding rose in her estimation.

He shrugged. "I suppose it was. But she's a very stubborn woman. I made her a very good offer, and she refused to think about it."

Mette didn't know how to reply to that. An offer? What could he mean?

"Well, I'd best be on my way," she said. "Thank you for the book you gave me…"

"Did you like it?"

She was a person who found it hard to tell a lie. "I find it somewhat…um…unrealistic…and the writing is…"

He laughed. She couldn't help noticing how straight his teeth were. Like a shelf of shoe boxes in the drapery. "You don't like it, in other words," he said. "Would you like to exchange it for one of Mr. Dickens' books?"

"I thought you said you didn't…"

"As it turns out, I have a complete set of his books. The Carleton's Illustrated Edition from 1873. They were tucked away in a corner. Would you like to come and take a look? You can pick the one you most want to read, and exchange it when you've finished. I suggest one of the shorter ones…A Christmas Carol, perhaps?"

She followed him into the house and to the most splendid room she had ever seen. Three walls were lined with books. A fireplace with a mantle made of Heart of Kauri filled the fourth side. Two large, brown, leather chairs faced the fireplace.

He pointed to the wall beside the door. "Here they are. See? Right down near the floor, on the lower shelves."

She knelt on the floor and opened the glass door of the lower shelf. There were at least ten books, all with identical red covers and gold print. She pulled out one of them—*The Old Curiosity Shop*—and opened it. The illustrations were beautiful. She ran her fingers over one showing an elderly gentleman with a walking stick being helped along by a young woman wearing a bonnet, a cloak draped over her shoulders.

"What's this one about?" she asked, turning to Mr. Harding and holding it up. He was leaning against the mantle watching her, with a strange look on his face.

"It's about an old man who gambles to help his beautiful young grand-daughter have a better life," he said. "She dies in the end, of course. Typical Dickens."

Mette returned the book to its place on the shelf, disappointed. She preferred not to know how a book ended. She pulled out another one. *Hard Times*. "Does anyone die in this one? No, don't tell me..."

"It's about the life of the imagination, more than anything," he said as she turned back to the shelf. "Romantic...do you like love stories, Mrs. Hardy?"

She heard him move closer and turned to find him kneeling on the floor behind her. He leaned forward as if to take the book from her hands, his face close to hers.

"I...I think I'd like to take this one please," she said. She tried to move away from him, but there was nowhere to go.

He leaned closer. "You can keep it if you like..."

"No, I don't need to..."

"You can keep them all. One a day for as long as you're here."

"One a day? What do you mean?"

"Come to my bed once a day for as long as you're in town, and each time I'll let you have another book."

She started to stand, sliding her back against the glass doors of the bookcases, but he grabbed her skirt and pulled her back down. She could feel his breath on her cheek. "Come here," he said, groping at her face. "Let me have a kiss."

She was still holding the book in her right hand. Without thinking about it too much, she lifted the book and slapped the spine hard against the side of his head. He swayed in place, then regained his balance. Bracing herself against the bookcase, she pushed hard against him with both hands. He sprawled backwards on the floor.

"I'm sorry Mr. Harding, but I have no idea why you think I might be interested in something like that." She stepped over him, her clogs knocking against his head, and marched from the room, first throwing the book on the ground beside his head. "I don't want any of your books, thank you."

"Stupid slut," he called after her. As she turned the handle of the front door, she heard him say, "The other one wouldn't go for it either. What's the matter with the women in this town. They don't know a decent offer when they hear one."

9

The Missing Man Kane

Frank stopped that night at Matamau, on the north side of the Forty Mile Bush. He could have pushed five or six miles further to the Scandinavian town of Norsewood and found a bed with one of Mette's many cousins, but darkness was falling and his horse was tired. Copenhagen was getting old—they both were—and it did no good to wear themselves out. With an early start the next day he could make it to Waipukurau in time to ask the younger Henry Monteith if Kane had given him a reason for selling his horse. Then he would push on to Waipawa to the Bank of New Zealand and see what the manager could tell him about the twenty pounds. Was it still there, or had Kane withdrawn it?

The Forty Mile Bush seemed more foreboding than when he had driven through on his coach. Perhaps it was because he was on horseback and more aware of the overhanging branches and the dark shadows between the massive trees. He saw few other travellers. A coach passed him heading towards Woodville, and a troop of mounted constables in bush uniform came out of the trees and galloped past him towards Napier without acknowledging his existence. Soon after they disappeared, he passed two men with swags on their backs who were plodding north. One was tall and stooped, the other short, more lively, taking long steps to keep up with the stride of his mate. They'd be looking for work, no doubt, like Peter Kane. The countryside was full of such men. Anyone who didn't have a regular job had to make do with short-term labouring jobs.

At the northern edge of the bush, he found a grassy spot just off the road by a stream, hidden between giant totara and tree ferns, and tossed down his bedroll. Copenhagen settled down to eat every blade she could reach.

He wasn't tired enough to attempt sleep. He left the campsite and followed the stream into the bush, mostly out of curiosity. About two hundred yards in he found another open area in the shadow of a steep, grassy slope, that would have made an even better campsite, but decided to remain where he was. He was not the first person to find the campsite. More than one campfire had been built here, and empty tins and matchboxes were strewn around. This was the sort of place that Peter Kane might have spent the night—away from the road and in the company of others. Swagmen often travelled together for safety.

He followed the stream back to his own campsite. Near the road, the setting sun hit something in the water. He waded in to see what it was. A watch. A large silver hunting watch. Not the kind of thing Peter Kane would have owned, but interesting even so. He put the watch in his pocket and returned to where he had left his horse, ate some food from his saddlebag, and settled down for the night.

He had the last three of the precious cigarettes he had been rationing since Mette had begged him to give them up, and decided now was the time to enjoy one of them. But all it did was stir up the cravings again, and he regretted it. Without thinking too much about it, he tossed the last two into the stream. They caught in an eddy and swirled away. The water was moving faster than he had realized, and he watched the cigarettes disappear, wishing he hadn't been so impulsive.

* * *

By noon, he was in Waipukurau, where the younger Monteith had his office. The town was small, unable to grow because it was surrounded by large pastoral stations. It had been founded a decade earlier as a model town by one man who had carefully selected the inhabitants, and it had the look of an English market town. Henry Monteith's office was near the railway station, a small building fronted by a brightly painted red door and a large window. His name and business details were painted on the lower half of the window: H. Monteith, Stock, Land, Estate, and General Commission Agent, Waipukurau. Goods Stored and Forwarded.

He found Henry Monteith, a youthful version of his father, with the same swept-back red hair, seated at an old pine desk, working on a leather-bound accounting ledger. He smiled at Frank and gestured towards a chair. "May I assist you, sir? Please, take a seat."

Frank sat down across the desk from him and offered Monteith his hand. "Hardy, Sergeant Frank Hardy. I'm searching for Peter Kane, who left Sandon a year ago. His wife..."

"He hasn't arrived home?" Monteith laid his pen in the fold of the accounts ledger and frowned. "I was wondering...he left here several months ago saying he'd be back in a few weeks."

"Why is that?" asked Frank. "Why was he intending to return?"

Monteith didn't answer immediately but flipped backwards through his accounting register. He found what he was looking for and tapped the page. "Ah, here it is. Twenty-five pounds. Yes. He'd put some money down on a piece of land...I'm the commission agent for land sales...and he assured me he'd be back soon after Christmas, with his wife and children, and would give me the final payment at that time. He said he had the money but not on him. He said he needed to pick it up, but didn't say from where. I assumed he'd sent it home. He owed another hundred pounds."

"He sold a horse to you," said Frank. If Kane had not had the full amount on him, the possibility that he'd hidden the rest of his money somewhere between Woodville and Waipukurau seemed more likely.

"Yes, he did. He was heading out to Mr. Nairn's Station at Pourerere, about twenty miles east of here, for the shearing season. He said he wouldn't need the horse while he was shearing. He felt it would be a drag on his expenses. He'd have had to pay for the feed and watering."

"Had he discovered the land he wanted when he sold you the horse?"

Monteith shook his head. "Not then. Not until he returned from shearing in mid-November. He said then that he'd found the perfect piece of land—ten acres that were on my books. He was excited about it. He said it reminded him of his birthplace in Tyrone. All rolling green hills with a view of the ocean in the distance."

"Mid November," said Frank. The murder in Woodville had occurred on November 22nd. "Was he headed home when he left here?"

"He went to Waipawa first, to the bank," said Monteith. "But he came back the same day and handed me the twenty-five pounds. I have it noted in my ledger as November 19th."

"Then he walked out of here towards home," said Frank. "Through The Forty Mile Bush."

"I believe so," said Monteith. "That's the route most people would take."

"Could he make it to Woodville on foot in four days?" asked Frank.

"Fifteen miles a day? I would think so," said Monteith. "Mind you, it was late in the day when he left. He'd already walked to Waipawa and back to get the money from the bank. He'd probably walk for two or three hours and find a place to stop. Then the second day—the twentieth—he'd be at the edge of the bush and he'd stop again."

"From there he could easily get to Woodville by the 22nd. of November," said Frank.

"Now I come to think of it, it was raining heavily at the time," said Monteith. "That would slow him down. We had two or three days of storms. It's possible he could have stopped somewhere and waited it out. I certainly would have if I were him. In which case he wouldn't make it to Woodville until after the 22nd."

"Hmm, it's certainly tight," said Frank. "Although not impossible."

"What's important about that date?" asked Monteith. "You're not thinking of the murder are you? He wasn't the type to commit a murder. He seemed like a very honest, hard-working man. And he was excited about seeing his wife and children again, and about bringing them back here. There's no reason to think he would suddenly become enraged and kill someone."

"I was thinking more that he was the reason for the murder. Or that he got mixed up with it accidentally. Your father told me he bought a lockbox at his store. He was carrying a considerable amount of money when he left home. We imagined that he decided to hide his money somewhere, which is why he only had twenty-five pounds to put down on the land he wanted." He stopped, thinking of something. "You paid him twenty-five pounds for the horse?"

"Twenty," said Monteith. "I had a big sale coming up and I knew I could turn it around for a quick profit."

"But he had twenty-five...I suppose he'd saved something from shearing," said Frank.

"I know he had more than twenty-five pounds on him," said Monteith. "But he wanted to keep some of it to take home. He said his wife would be running out. He'd sent her some a month or so earlier. Actually, he offered me something else as surety, but I turned it down. A watch."

Frank slid the watch he had found from his pocket. "Not this watch?" he asked.

Monteith took the watch and turned it over in his hands. "I can't swear to it, but it was certainly very similar to this one," he said. "A hunting watch, I believe. He said it was left to him by an uncle."

Heavy rain, a campsite beside a stream...had what happened to Kane not been connected with the murder at all? Had he been swept away by a fresh—a rush of water coming down from the hills after heavy rain? He wouldn't be the first person to lose his life that way. But in that case, why wasn't his body somewhere along the banks of the stream?

He could continue on to Waipawa and ask the bank manager about the deposit. But that had been explained. What he needed to do now was take another look at that stream, to see if there was any other sign that Kane had been there. Then, if nothing turned up, he would return to Woodville and take one last shot at discovering whether Kane had made it back there in time for the murder. Perhaps if he heard Samuel Kemp out on what was bothering him, Kemp would point him in a useful direction.

"Could I take the deposit back to Mrs. Kane?" he asked.

Monteith thought for a minute, then shook his head. "I'd like to trust you, but it's my duty to make sure the money gets to the right person," he said.

"Tell Mrs. Kane that if she sends me a notarized letter I'll forward the twenty-five pounds to her."

As Frank left, Monteith uttered the usual warning about swagmen in the Forty Mile Bush. Remembering the two swagmen he had seen on the way through the bush, Frank shrugged. They were harmless, most of them. Tired, hungry, and wanting nothing more than some work to sustain themselves for a few more weeks. No reason to be afraid.

10

The Slip

The sun was hovering just above the horizon when he arrived back at the edge of the Forty Mile Bush. He left Copenhagen in the same spot as the previous night, and walked upstream once more, this time paying careful attention to his surroundings at every step. The stream was down to a trickle, but he could see signs of previous freshes, sudden rushes of water after rain, that had torn away trees and turned the banks to mounds of mud. On one side of the stream, a cliff jutted up above the trees, sheltering the campsite. A flash flood would trap anyone using the site between the edge of the stream and the cliff.

He searched the second campsite thoroughly, looking for the smallest hint of the presence of Peter Kane. He found a billy can with a hole in the bottom, which could have belonged to anyone. And not far away from the billy, he found a treasure—a packet of Old Kents with one lone cigarette inside. He stuffed the package in his pocket. He would save it for when he really needed it. It would definitely be his last one.

There was still enough light for him to search further upstream. He rounded a bend and found himself at the foot of a long grassy slope. The stream had disappeared underground and would reappear further on. The slope looked as if it was the result of an old slide; it ended fifty yards above him with a short rise to the ridge that ran alongside the creek. A lone tree, its branches gnarled and dead, bent by strong northeasterly winds that came down from the ranges, sat at the pinnacle of the slope.

The distinctiveness of the tree gave him an idea. If he wanted to hide something, he'd need to find a memorable place, somewhere that stood out in bush with a million similar trees. This elevated spot, and this unusual tree, offered an ideal hiding place.

He climbed the slope, noticing how soft it was. It wouldn't take much to bring it down, and he stopped short, wondering if he was being foolish. If the hill collapsed again he could be buried under the soil and rocks, his corpse so well hidden it would never be found. That would leave Mette in the same position as Mrs. Kane. But the desire to find the truth drove him upwards. He'd found the spot, in his heart he was sure.

Near the top of the slope, almost as high up as the crowns of the larger trees surrounding the base of the hill, he saw something metallic sticking up out of the dirt. It was no more than a yard from the base of the tree. A tin lid with a handle. He sat beside it and eased it from its hiding place. In a few minutes, the object was in his hands. A lockbox. The front of the lockbox bore the mark of a rock. Someone had attempted to smash it open while it was still half-buried. The marks looked recent but the lock had held. He would take it back to Mr. Monteith in Woodville and ask him if it was the one he had sold to Peter Kane. Then he would give it to Mrs. Kane, who could find a locksmith to force it open.

He rose to his feet, ready to make his way down the slope, the lockbox in hand when a voice spoke from behind him.

"Hey, you."

He turned. A tall, thin man, wearing a cloth coat several sizes too large for him, was standing at the top of the slope, glaring at him. He held a crowbar in one hand.

"That's my lockbox you have there."

For a minute, Frank thought it might be Peter Kane standing above him, but the man was tall—over six feet—and had light-coloured hair. A swagman.

"If this is your lockbox, why are you holding a crowbar?" he asked. He was confident the swagman would not be able to take the lockbox from him.

"It's mine because I found it," said the man. "I found it earlier today and went to find a crowbar. I'm walking and I couldn't carry it..."

"We're sharing it," said a voice from the bottom of the slope. "He has a crowbar and I have a gun."

Frank turned slowly. Too late he remembered seeing the tall man walking through the bush with his shorter companion. The second of the two men, the short one, held an old duelling pistol in one hand, pointing it at Frank. From forty yards away Frank could see the pistol shake as the swagman tried to hide his nervousness. It was a gun he knew from his childhood—an old Wogden and Barton with a hair-trigger. The most famous duelling pistol in Britain—famous because shooters rarely missed. He'd need to be careful with this one. The man could easily shoot him accidentally, with his finger trembling on the trigger.

He placed the lockbox on the ground, setting off a small shower of stones down the slope, put his hands up, and sat on the dirt at an angle so he could keep an eye on the man with the crowbar. "Is it loaded?"

"Of course it is," said the man with the crowbar. "It's loaded, isn't it Jimmy?"

The man with the gun nodded. "Yeah. It's loaded." He waved the gun at Frank. "Stand up and bring me the lockbox," he said. "And don't make any sudden moves."

"Have you cleaned the gun lately?" asked Frank, staying where he was. "You know, an old gun like that isn't likely to perform well if it hasn't been cleaned. And you'll only have one shot. You should have brought the pair with you. Chances are, you'll miss, especially with a smooth bore. If you shoot and miss, I'll come down there and take it from you. You won't like it."

The man holding the gun looked at his companion at the top of the hill and nodded. Frank heard a click as he threw himself sideways. He felt dirt and stones spraying as the bullet hit inches from his head. The sound reached him a second later, deafening him.

Before either man could move, he was on his feet and sliding down the slope towards the man with the pistol. But as he did, the ground started to move. Either the bullet itself or the explosive sound of the shot had stirred the mass of earth. He lost his footing and fell backwards.

Feet first, lying on his back, he began to slide rapidly downhill, his hands clawing at the ground for purchase. The man with the gun disappeared under the slip without a sound. He felt himself sinking into the liquefying ground, and made an effort to tuck himself into a ball, his arms holding his knees. As he spun around he saw the trees below coming at him fast and braced himself for the hit.

Something hard banged against his head, and he lost consciousness briefly; he came to as he was slammed against the trunk of a massive totara tree. The air was filled with dust, blocking out the last sunshine of the day. The lockbox had disappeared. Any money inside was probably gone forever. But he was above the slip, not beneath it.

Looking back, he could see the tree at the top of the slope still standing, tilting slightly. The man who had been up there had disappeared. He scanned the hillside for signs of life but could see nothing.

He rolled away from the tree and felt a sharp stab of pain in his arm and shoulder. When he tried to lift his arm, it refused his command and hung uselessly by his side. He'd dislocated his shoulder. Moving it even slightly with his other hand sent waves of pain through his right side.

The nearest doctor would be either twenty miles north or forty miles south, and there was no guarantee that the doctor would be in his surgery. Doctors in bush country were regularly called out to help injured people, especially with all the forestry and road building going on in this area. He knew it was important to reduce a dislocation as quickly as possible after the event. He'd seen it happen to men during battle. He sat for a few minutes, breathing deeply, calming himself, knowing it was going to hurt.

Carefully, he lifted his numb right arm with his left hand and lay it across his raised knee. Then, grunting with the pain, he locked his hands together tightly in front of his knees and began to lean slowly backwards.

The pain was excruciating, and he was almost blinded by the sweat running down his forehead. But a pop presaged a sudden alleviation from the pain, and his arm slowly came back to life. He stood and moved his arm gently back and forward, flexing his fingers. It felt as if it had snapped back into place. Thank God for that. Riding back to Woodville was going to be awkward. He'd have to keep his arm still to make sure it didn't jolt out of place again. But that would have to wait until tomorrow. For now, he needed a good night's sleep.

He staggered back to the campsite where he'd left Copenhagen. She was standing in the same spot, having devoured all the grass in the area; she looked at him accusingly.

"Sorry old girl," he said. "I was detained."

Then he propped his bedroll against the trunk of a totara tree and leaned back, after first making a rough sling out of his belt to stop his arm flopping around while he slept and doing further damage. His gun was still in his coat pocket, but he doubted the two men were going to come at him again. They'd been taken by the earth. He fell asleep instantly.

* * *

Woodville was stirring as he rode in the next morning. He had awoken before the sun was up, eaten a sparse breakfast, splashed his face with the muddy waters of the stream, still showing the effects of the slip, and headed through the bush along the rutted gravelled track between the massive trees. He'd made another search for the bodies of the two men but again had seen no sign of them—not even a boot or hat thrown free by the slip. They were gone. Later he would send someone to dig for them and tell them to keep an eye out for the lockbox. But with his damaged shoulder he could do nothing himself.

The Forty Mile Bush ran almost all the way to Woodville. As he neared town he saw a number of clearings where Scandinavian immigrants were hacking out farms. Smoke drifted from tree stumps, and the sound of hammering filled the air. He felt a sudden longing to be back on his farm, pulling out tree stumps and building his house, with Mette by his side.

In Woodville, the town clustered around a single street, with a few homes on parallel streets on either side of the main street.

A group of men had gathered outside Fountaine and Monteith's general store. Monteith saw Frank arriving and hurried towards him. He looked worried.

"Sergeant Hardy. Did you meet my son?"

"I did, and he was most helpful. What's going on here?"

"We're about to search for Samuel Kemp. He was in Mr. Murphy's hotel last night and speaking as if he intended self-harm. He's been upset lately and believes he's suffering from something in his head. A demon. This morning Mr. Murphy realized that one of his rifles was missing. The one he keeps behind the bar. He went to check on Kemp in the Accommodation House, where he usually sleeps, worrying about Kemp's intentions. He's not there and we can't find him anywhere in town."

"I'll come and help you search," said Frank, feeling guilty that he hadn't listened to Kemp before he left town. "Where might he be, do you think?"

Monteith glanced back at the group. "Some of the men in the hotel last night heard him say something about a lie he'd told, a lie about the murder. But he didn't say what the lie was and they all assumed it was to do with him saying Harry Thomsen said he saw the body when he shouldn't have been able to. But other people heard what Thomsen said, so how it could have been a lie... now we're wondering if he was involved in the murder itself. The police found blood on the pillow where George Ollandt slept the night before, and they did wonder if he was killed in his room."

"But there were signs that he'd been splitting palings and that the handle of his maul had broken," said Frank. "Doesn't it seem more likely that he was killed in the bush, and the body moved? It'd be hard to find the murder site in this bush. It's so dense..."

"True," said Monteith. "But something was bothering Kemp. He spoke about demons in his head that wouldn't stay quiet. Do you think your fellow—Peter Kane—was there and helped Harry for some reason. His body could even be..."

Frank shook his head. "I think I can discount that theory," he said. "I believe Kane was buried by a landslide on his way back to Woodville. There's no body, but there's some evidence he was there where a slip occurred."

The men in the group started to move. "We're heading out to the murder site," one called out. "We think that's where he'd go if he wanted to harm himself."

"Leave your horse here," Monteith said to Frank. "It's a twenty-minute walk, and not easy on horseback."

Frank tethered his horse to the hitching post in front of the store, difficult to achieve with one arm pinned to his side. Then he joined the searchers. They spread out two deep across a track that only they could see. The bush was thick and filled with fallen or felled trees, broken branches, and vines. It was hard going, and Frank's shoulder started to throb.

They were fifteen minutes into their walk when the sound of a gunshot echoed through the trees.

"Kemp," said one of the men. "He's done himself in."

As one, the men began to stumble through the undergrowth in the direction from which the sound had come.

They found Kemp, his back pressed against the tree beside the place Ollandt's body had been found. The rifle was clutched in his hands, still pointing towards where his head had once been. He had removed his boot and attached his big toe to the trigger of the rifle with a piece of flax. Then he had put the barrel in his mouth and pulled the trigger with his toe. A letter covered with fragments of blood and bone lay on his lap.

One of the men, braver than the others, took a closer look at the blood-splattered tree. "There's a ball wedged in the trunk," he said. "Right above the centre of his head...well, what used to be his head."

"Did he do it on purpose?" someone asked.

The man at the tree stood back from the body. "Course he did," he said. "Look how he's holding the rifle. And look at the toe with the flax. You think that happened by accident? He's left a letter here as well. No doubt, it's a suicide. Better get the doctor and Constable Gillespie."

Frank felt sick. Why had he not stopped to listen to Samuel Kemp? He bent over and took some deep breaths. Mr. Murphy, the hotel owner came over and put his hand on Frank's shoulder, unintentionally causing a stab of pain.

"Are you all right, sergeant?" he asked.

Frank shook his head. "He wanted to talk to me about something," he said. "And I..."

"He tried to talk to all of us," said Murphy. "Don't upset yourself. He wasn't right in the head anymore. Nothing anyone could do to stop him."

"What about the murder?"

Murphy shrugged. "It's clear that Harry killed George. It's clear to me, at least. And he got away with it. But fate has a way of catching up with people who disregard the laws of the land. God sees to that."

Frank knew that wasn't always the way, but said nothing. It was over. This case had nothing to do with him. He had found as much as he was going to find about Peter Kane. Time to let it all go.

He returned alone to town, his arm aching and his head throbbing. Thoughts of his dead brother were flooding through his mind. His brother Will, who had deserted to the enemy all those years ago during the Land Wars, and lost his head because of it. The sight of another man with his head blown away had brought the memories rushing back.

He climbed awkwardly onto Copenhagen and spurred her towards home. Time to get back to Mette and a normal life. No more adventure. No more sleeping rough and eating badly. He was done with it. Time to be a man, start a family and settle down properly.

11

The Last One

Mette was angry with Mr. Harding but even angrier with herself. She did not even like the man but had gone to his house to see his library because she was enthralled by the idea of seeing all those books. She hadn't stopped to think for one minute that she was going to look exactly like Mrs. Johnston to anyone who saw her.

What would Frank think if he heard she had gone to visit a man she barely knew in his own home, by herself? She knew he trusted her, but would he think she'd been foolish? Or worse?

She strode towards Mr. Tomlinson's house, thinking desperately. What was she going to tell Frank? Should she keep it all a secret and risk someone else telling him that they'd seen her? Or should she confess her error to him immediately and risk his anger—or at least his annoyance. At least she still had some time. He'd only been away for a few days, and might not return for another week. For the first time since she had arrived, she was happy he wasn't with her.

As she turned the corner, she saw a familiar horse in front of the store. Copenhagen! Forgetting all her problems she broke into a run.

Frank was sitting in one of Mr. Tomlinson's chairs, his coat off, with a strange man wrapping some kind of sheeting around his arm. His face split into a broad grin when he saw her come through the door.

"Mette. Here you are. I was ready to comb the town for you."

"What happened to your arm?"

The man wrapping Frank's arm turned and nodded at her. "Mrs Hardy? I'm Dr. Johnston. Sergeant Hardy and I met on the way to Woodville recently. Your husband dislocated his shoulder, and I'm putting it in a sling. Come here and I'll show you what to do. The sling will need to come off for washing every few days and you'll have to put it back on."

Mette stood close to Frank, her hand resting on his unencumbered shoulder, and watched as the doctor explained his wrapping system. She could feel Frank looking up at her, and stole a look at him. The look in his eyes set her heart pounding with worry. Mr. Harding was prowling through her mind again, with all his nasty suggestiveness.

"I believe I met your wife," she said to the doctor, tearing her eyes from Frank's. "I was watching a cricket match yesterday, and we sat together."

"Just the two of you?" he asked, not looking at her.

"Um, yes," she said cautiously. Did Dr. Johnston know his wife had been visiting the local hotel with a strange man? "We sat on the grass together."

"I suppose Mr. Moore was playing in the match," said the doctor.

"I...I'm not sure," said Mette. "I don't know many people here yet."

The doctor made a humphing sound as he tore the end of the sheet into two strips and tied the final knot. "That should keep your arm secure, Sergeant Hardy. Now try to keep it as still as possible."

"How long should I wear this thing?" asked Frank.

"At least two weeks," said Dr. Johnston. "While your wife washes it, make sure you're doing something relaxing. Reading the newspaper or taking your dog for a walk, for example. No climbing over fences or throwing sticks for your dog fetch. And keep it still."

"We don't have a dog," said Frank. "But I'll need to ride my horse occasionally or she'll start to stiffen up. I'll make sure I'm wearing the sling when I ride."

"Good," said Dr. Johnston. "And remember, even after two weeks, you'll need to be careful for a month or so. No hammering, or lifting anything heavy. If you dislocate your shoulder again it could become chronic and you'll be unable to do any physical work for the rest of your life. Are you right-handed?"

Frank nodded. "I suppose I can still do some things with my left hand," he said. "That won't matter, will it?"

The doctor glanced at Mette and Frank, pressed closely together, Mette squeezing Frank's undamaged shoulder. "You can," he said. "But be careful. And don't do anything that will create leverage. No leaning on your elbows for example."

Mette blushed as she realized the implication of what the doctor was saying. She caught Frank's eye and tried to look away. He was grinning happily.

"I'm sure I'll be able to avoid that somehow," he said.

"Did you find what happened to Peter Kane," asked Mette, mainly to change the subject.

"I think so," said Frank. He stood up. "I believe he died in a slip. The same slip that threw me down a slope and dislocated my arm. I found a couple of his belongings at the site. A watch and a lockbox. I'd like to talk with Mrs. Kane and explain what I think happened. There's some good news as well. Kane made a downpayment on a piece of land, and she can get the money back if she sends him a notarized letter. It isn't much—twenty-five pounds—but I'm sure it will help."

"I spoke with her this morning, and..."

Mr. Tomlinson came from the back of the store, where he'd been stocking his shelves. "Back so soon, Sergeant Hardy?

Frank gave a quick explanation of what he had discovered. "We're going to see Mrs. Kane," he said. "I'll come back afterwards and you can decide what you owe me."

Frank slung his coat over his shoulders and he and Mette left the store. Outside, as soon as they were out of sight of the doctor and Mr. Tomlinson, he stopped to give her a quick kiss. "I missed you," he said. "I'm not as keen on adventure and living rough as I thought I was. I'm afraid I've already been ruined."

His turn of phrase jolted Mette. She'd better tell him about Mr. Harding now before he heard something from someone else. She crossed her fingers and plunged in. "I met someone here who has a whole library of books," she began. "Actually, he knocked me out of the dray when we first arrived."

"He did?" Frank stopped walking and frowned. "You mean he attacked you?"

"No. He was driving too fast and made Mr. Tomlinson's dray horse jump sideways. Anyway, he lent me a book—which I didn't like very much—and I saw him just now in the street and told him so. He asked me to come into his house and pick another book. And I did."

Frank looked angry. "What did he do, Mette. Tell me and I'll go and kill him."

Mette knew Frank wasn't exactly speaking in an exaggerated way. He had killed for her before. So she said quickly, "He didn't DO anything. It was what he said. He asked me to go into his bedroom with him, and when I refused he was very rude...I felt..."

Franks' expression softened. "You were worried about what I might think if I found out, weren't you?" he asked. "Especially considering the way Mrs. Johnston has been behaving. You don't need to worry. I trust you."

She let out her breath, which she hadn't realized she had been holding. "Yes, I was. I felt so stupid. Mr. Tomlinson warned me against him, and when I saw him—Mr. Harding—try to cheat at cricket..."

Frank laughed. "He went that low? My God, he must...did you say Harding? You don't mean Cyril Harding, do you? Colonel Feilding's blue-eyed boy?"

Mette hadn't intended to mention his name, but it was out now so she nodded. "You know him?"

"Not very well. I've run into him at volunteer recruitment meetings in Palmerston. He seemed like a pompous fool." He started walking again. "A handsome fool, I suppose."

"Not as handsome as you," said Mette. "And quite ugly inside."

"I'm not going to worry about him," said Frank. "And neither should you. But if he does anything more to upset you I'll challenge him to a duel..." He saw the look on Mette's face and stopped. "No, I'll challenge him to a boxing match and ruin his pretty face."

"Not until your shoulder is better," said Mette.

Frank laughed. "He's safe for a couple of months, then," he said. He squeezed her arm. "And we're going to have to work out how to get around the 'no leaning on my elbows' rule."

Mette giggled. She liked Frank making jokes like that. It felt naughty, especially in daylight.

They walked together to Mrs. Kane's house, arm in arm, chatting about their time apart. Mette was shocked by the details of the murder in Woodville. She'd been there shortly after it happened, and thought she might have seen Harry Thomsen when he returned after the trial and tried to get people to stay at the Accommodation House. She'd seen swagmen ignore him and continue on to Mr. Murphy's hotel, even though it was a lot more expensive. He must have left town since then.

"How awful that Samuel Kemp felt he had to shoot himself," she said when Frank reached the end of his story. "Did it remind you of Will?"

He nodded. "Yes, it did. Although my brother didn't die by his own hand. But the head..."

They walked the rest of the way in silence, Mette stroking Frank's arm. She had seen him wake up after a nightmare, pale and sweating, but he was hardly ever sad during the day.

Mrs. Kane was in the back garden, taking down the washing. She nodded at Mette and kept working, her thin hands flashing in and out of the peg bag tied around her waist.

Mette went and stood beside her.

"Mary," she said softly. "My husband—this is my husband Frank—has returned with news of your husband. Would you like to sit down so we can talk?"

Mary Kane looked around tiredly. "I have no chairs in the house. There's only that branch over there, where Peter and I used to..." She sat down on the willow branch they had sat on earlier. Mette sat beside her and took her hand. Frank knelt in front of them both.

"Mary...you don't mind if I call you Mary, do you?"

She shook her head. "Did you find Peter?"

"I traced him from Waipukurau, where he visited a land agent," said Frank.

"He'd been up to Waipawa to withdraw twenty pounds from the Bank of New Zealand. He'd been shearing at Mr. Nairn's station at Pourerere and felt an attraction to the area. He left twenty-five pounds with Mr. Monteith, the land agent, to hold a nice piece of land. He told Monteith that it was hilly, with a view of the ocean, and that it reminded him of Tyrone."

Mary Kane smiled. "That sounds like Peter," she said. "He loved Tyrone, even though he hadn't seen it since he was young. He was in Australia, you know..."

"But he told Monteith—the land agent—that he was coming home to fetch you and the children, and that he had to pick up the rest of the money as well."

"He should have had the money with him," said Mary Kane. "He always carried it..."

"He purchased a lockbox from Mr. Monteith—the father of the land agent—when he was passing through Woodville," said Frank. "And I found a lockbox at the site of an old slip, just north of the Forty Mile Bush. But I lost it in a second slip."

Mary Kane's lips tightened into a line. "That could have belonged to anyone," she said.

Frank reached awkwardly into his pocket with his left hand and pulled out the watch. "I found this at the slip as well," he said. "It was in the water..."

Mary Kane did not look at the watch, but stared at the ground, her face stricken. "The last one," she said.

Frank moved back to see what she was staring at. The package of Old Kents had fallen from his pocket and lay on the ground between them. He picked it up. "You recognize this package?"

She nodded and took it from him, blinking away tears. "He always carried a package of Old Kents, with one cigarette in it. He didn't want to smoke—he said it cost too much. But he said if he had the last one on him it would always be the last one as long as he didn't smoke it."

"I found it near the watch," he said. "There's only one cigarette inside. It was going to be my last one as well."

"Do you have the lockbox? Was the money still in it?" asked Mette.

He shook his head. "I had it, but it disappeared in the slip." He refrained from mentioning the two men. He would let Constable Gillespie know what had happened, in case they had families waiting for them somewhere.

"Perhaps someone robbed him," said Mette. "And left the watch and the cigarette package there." She wasn't sure if she should be giving Mary Kane hope that her husband might be alive somewhere, but she couldn't help herself.

Mary Kane sat up straighter, her face brightening. "Yes. Yes. Maybe that's what happened, but..." She slumped again. "But who would steal a single cigarette from someone."

"I believe he's under the slip," said Frank. "It would have been very fast. I doubt he even had a chance to know what was happening." He stood up and offered his hand to Mary Kane. "Mr. Tomlinson will help you retrieve the funds from Monteith. The money that your husband left with him for the down payment..."

"But if he comes home, he'll be upset that he's lost the land."

Frank and Mette exchanged glances. Mette put her arms around Mary Kane. "You should probably accept that he died in the slip," she said. "And start thinking about your children. Perhaps you could use some of the money Mr. Tomlinson has raised to go to California and start a new life with your brother."

She shook her head. "What would he think if he came home and I was gone? No, I'll wait for a while...a long while. I just don't believe he's dead."

And with that, they had to be content.

* * *

Mr. Tomlinson insisted on giving Frank the full fifty pounds and took him to the paddock behind the store to see the broodmare he had promised Frank.

"This is Dolores," he said. "She has several more years of fertility, and she'll give you some excellent offspring if you mate her with the right stallion."

Mette looked deep into Dolores' soft brown eyes and fell in love instantly. "How will we get her to the farm?" she asked.

"I'll tie a guide rope to my saddle and we'll lead her there," said Frank. He looked at Mette, who was stroking Dolores' mane. "How are you at knots?"

"I can tie knots," she said. "I grew up in a port city. Everyone there could tie knots."

"I learn something new about you every day," said Frank. "What other talents do you have that you haven't mentioned?"

"I can use a hammer," she said. "I've been wanting to help you build the house, but you were enjoying it so much I hated to mention it."

"We can do it together," said Frank. "I'll do the heavy lifting with my good arm, and you can hammer the planks into place." He saw her trying to hide a smile, and added, "I suppose you think you can do the lifting as well, don't you?"

Mr. Tomlinson sighed impatiently. "You can take the mare home with you then? Excellent. I'll get a rope for you from the house."

He returned a few minutes later holding a flyer. "I had forgotten about this. Mr. Morley will have his stud-horse Bryan O'Lynn standing in Palmerston all next week," he said. "In the paddock behind the Royal Hotel. And I think Dolores is due to be in heat any day now. It'll cost you five pounds, but he's a decent horse. A seven-year-old dapple bay, who stands 16 3/4 hands. You'd have your first sale by early next year. A good one, I would say."

They left Sandon and rode towards the farm, Mette sitting in front of Frank, while Dolores plodded happily behind them as if she too was heading home.

"Did we solve anything?" he asked after a while.

"Of course we did," said Mette. "We have money, we have a mare with a future, and you're going to let me help you build our house. You don't want to go off on adventures and sleep rough anymore." She paused for a minute until honesty overcame her. "And I learned that having a husband who shares your exact interests is less important than..."

"...having one who is loyal and loves you," said Frank. "Which is what you have."

12

1914: The Death of Mrs Kane

In 1914, the local newspapers reported on the death of Mrs. Mary Kane, whose husband had gone missing thirty-five years previously.

From Our Own Correspondent I have to thank the Secretary of the Sandon Old Boys' Association for furnishing me with the information of the death at Palo Alto, California, on December 29th of Mrs Mary Kane, aged 69. This news will be received with more than the usual affectionate interest by those who remember deceased as a resident of Sandon 35 years ago and how hard she worked to maintain and educate her daughter "Winnie" and her two boys "Pat" and "Tom." How and under what circumstances deceased was widowed while a resident of Sandon so long ago is one of those tragic mysteries that has yet to be solved. Mr Kane left home to seek work and was employed in the Woodville and Pahiatua districts, where, being steady and industrious, he was known to have accumulated a considerable sum of money with which he expressed his intention to return to his wife and family. But he did not reach them and from that time to this he has been lost to human ken. For long years the wife and. children waited for husband and father, believing always that he would return to them if living, and after patient police search and long continued faith and inquiry, the "if living" became more sadly significant. The Sandon people of those, days—as through all the subsequent days, were kind and sympathetic and they sought, in various ways, to help the widow and the orphans, but mother preferred to fight her own hard battle and resented every attempt to financially assist her or to improve her environment. Of such stiff and sturdy stuff heroines are made, but it repels ordinary intimacy. Having relatives in California the late Mrs Kane decided to join them. This proved to be a wise decision, for in that sunny land fortune smiled upon this remarkable mother and her notable children. The former's epistles to me in the years that are gone indicated an education beyond her position, and I often wondered how a woman who laboured so hard with her hands could write and form such beautiful letters. To her children Mrs Donovan (nee Winifred Kane), "Pat" and "Tom," all of whom are old pupils of the Sandon School, I tender the deep sympathy of all who knew them and "mother" thirty-five years ago.

Rangitikei Advocate and Manawatu Argus, Rangitikei Advocate and Manawatu Argus, Volume XXXIX, Issue 10875, 13 February 1914

THE END

13

Frank and Mette: The Backstories

The backstories of Frank and Mette are sprinkled throughout the Sergeant Frank Hardy Mysteries. However, I have a fuller picture in my head, from which I draw as I write. Without giving any spoilers, here's what's in my mind.

Sergeant Frank Hardy

First, what does Frank look like? Think of the actor Clive Standen, born on a British Army base in Ireland, who plays Rollo in *Vikings*, and former FBI agent Bryan Mills in *Taken*. At 38, and six foot two tall, I'd happily cast Standen as Frank in a Netflix series of my books (Just dreaming! Won't happen). He'd have to wear brown contact lenses, however, as Frank is darker than most Englishman because he has Spanish blood; his father met his Spanish mother during the Peninsula War in Spain. Note that Frank's horse, Copenhagen, is named for the Duke Of Wellington's horse. Find photos of Clive Standen at IMBD.

Sergeant Frank Hardy is an ex-Die Hard - a British soldier of the 57th Regiment of Foot. The 57th Regiment arrived in New Zealand in 1860, after fighting in India and Crimea. They were sent there to fight in the Taranaki Wars, which began in my hometown, Waitara, in the province of Taranaki. The regiment left New Zealand in 1867 and Frank joined the Armed Constabulary. An interesting fact about this group is that they wore blanket kilts when they fought in the bush. Perhaps that's why some of Diana Gabaldon's fans have read my books.

During the last few years of the 1860s, a charismatic leader named Titokowaru arose in southern Taranaki in the area of my second hometown, Patea. (My father was a bank manager and we moved around a lot). Titokowaru's rebellion was in response to a brutal campaign by the British Army, who marched through Taranaki destroying villages and killing Maori. The atrocity that opens Not the Faintest Trace actually occurred in that period. I read about it in the wonderful book, I Shall Not Die: Titokowaru's War by James Belich. I changed the name of the colonial soldier responsible for the atrocity, who was later given the New Zealand Cross for another action. Frank's disgust with the event, and what later happened to his brother (also based on real events) led to where we find him in the first book: living in a small Scandinavian settlement in Palmerston (later named Palmerston North), bored and unhappy. This leads us to Mette.

Mette Jensen

In *Not the faintest Trace*, Mette is described as being tall, blond, and not as pretty as her shorter, plumper sister. I think of her as someone we would now consider as attractive. She is physically stronger and more athletic than her contemporaries. She is also fitter than smoker Frank, and able to run longer distances than he can without taking a rest. See *Recalled to Life* for that story. I would cast Swedish actress Alicia Vikander in her role. She was in —appropriately—*The Danish Girl*—and also in *Ex Machina* and *Tomb Raider*.

At 22, Mette is several years younger than Frank. She is from Haderslev, which was once situated in the Duchy of Schleswig. Schleswig was a bone of contention between Denmark and Germany for many years, and ownership moved back and forth between the two countries. In the early 1870s, during the Franco-Prussian War, men from Schleswig were inducted forcibly into the Prussian Army. As many of them felt they were Danish and not German they began to leave for other countries. That was why my own great grandparents left Denmark for New Zealand in 1874. Mette and her sister Maren arrived later, driven by the lack of men in Schleswig, and by the death of their father and brother in the Franco-Prussian War in 1870-71.

Mette is interested in both the people and the flora and fauna of New Zealand. She writes a small cookbook which is sold in the bookshop in Palmerston where she works. Eventually, her books will make the family wealthy, but so far, Frank and Mette are just barely scraping out a living.

If you read this section, thanks. There's more about the Danes in New Zealand on my website: www.wendymwilson.com

14

Glossary of Maori Words

Although I may not have used all these words in each book, they have all been used at some point. I try to make them understandable in context but that is not always possible. Maori place names can also be tricky as it's hard to read about places when you can't pronounce them. If you really want to know, I suggest you try Google Translate or The Maori Dictionary, which you will find online The latter is an excellent resource.

- **The Marae**: A meeting area in front of the meeting house.
- **The Pa**, a fortified Maori village. The Pa in this book does not exist. I used the original Maori name of Palmerston for the name of the Pa. The fact that Hakopa sold the Pa without the consent of his tribe was something that did actually happen, as land was communal. Note that Hakopa is the Maori version of Jacob, a reference to the biblical story of Jacob and Esau. Esau was the one who gave up the land for a mess of pottage, but there's no Maori equivalent for that name.
- **Whare**: A Maori hut made of flax or bullrushes.
- **Pakeha**: White or European New Zealanders. The term is still used in New Zealand on government websites and is not generally considered racist in the country.
- **Turehu**: A white ghost with red hair. I have exaggerated the importance of this ghost in Maori mythology, mostly because Jens had red hair and I

wanted an equivalent to the Scandinavian troll.

- **Haka**: A war dance with actions. Usually done before rugby games these days. YouTube has several performed by the All Black, the New Zealand rugby team. You'll love them.
- **Powhiri**: The greeting ceremony performed when dignitaries arrive at a Pa. You can see a nervous Hilary Clinton being welcomed with a powhiri when she was Secretary of State. Look for it on YouTube.
- **Tapu**: Taboo, or forbidden, because something is sacred.
- **Hangi**: A feast cooked in a hole with hot rocks and leaves. I once attended a hangi where a group of ad executives cooked a roast pig using this method. When it was taken out the pig was not fully cooked, which made things awkward as you can't really put it back in for an extra hour. Fortunately my agency also represented Alka Seltzer.
- **Hongi**: Not to be confused with hangi. The act of touching noses as a greeting. Watch various members of the Royal Family do this on YouTube.
- **Waka**: A dugout canoe. A small waka is called a waka teti. Teti means basket, so presumably a waka teti is a basket-sized canoe, although not shaped that way.
- **Utu**: Can mean revenge, but the meaning is closer to balance or equaling out.
- **Wiremu**: Karira's first name is Wiremu, the Maori name for William. Maori names often come from a Maori pronunciation of the English name, so Hori is George, Hohepa is Joseph, and Hemi is James. In the second book you will meet Wiki, short for Wikitoria, or Victoria.

15

Frank and Mette Meet

Frank and Mette first meet in Not the Faintest Trace. Because you have read this novella, you know they eventually married and this chapter will not be a spoiler. Here is the chapter where Mette first meets Frank:

Chapter Three: The Forager

At last, after four days of unrelenting rain, the skies had cleared and a thin spring sun had started to dry the mud. Mette Jensen took the opportunity to do some washing in the iron tub in front of the cottage, enjoying the warmth of the sun as she did. Days since Paul Nissen and her cousin, Jens, the boy she had grown up with and loved like a brother, had gone missing, and no one had any idea where they might be. She was awash in sorrow.

What could have become of them? She missed them terribly. They were the only two other young people she could talk to in Palmerston, and now she had no one except her younger sister, Maren, who was preoccupied with her husband and young son Hamlet. Everyone had thought Mette would marry Paul Nissen, although he was three years younger than she was. He was tall and strong, and nice to look at, but a boy. She preferred to wait for the right man, and she knew Paul was not that man, as much as she liked him.

Maren came out of the cottage and called to her.

"Mette, what are you doing?"

"I'm finishing the washing," she said. "Then I'm going into the bush to find some fresh greens."

Maren waddled towards her, one hand on her growing belly, looking anxious.

"I wish you wouldn't go into the forest," she said. "I'm scared for you."

Mette smiled. "Maren, there's nothing to worry about. The bush is beautiful and I love to go there."

"I'm afraid a pack of wild Hauhau will catch you and kill you and eat you for dinner," said Maren.

"I'm sure I'll be delicious," said Mette. "I'll make sure they save a piece for…" She stopped as Maren's eyes filled with tears. "Please, don't worry about me, Maren dear. I'll be quite safe and will stay on the path where I can run home quickly. If I scream loud enough the men will hear me from the mill and come running."

Maren sighed and returned to the cottage. Mette wrung out her apron and hung it to dry over a knot of scrub that sprang to life in place of the trees the men had felled. The apron was getting thin as she had brought it with her from Haderslev two years ago, but she loved the red and gold embroidery that her mother had stitched so carefully on the two aprons, giving one to her and the other to Maren. Holding it made her feel like she was home again, sitting in her mother's kitchen eating *aebleskiver*, her lips coated with sugar. Sugar! If she could have some real sugar just once, that would be wonderful. Powdered sugar would be even better. She might kill someone for a taste of powdered sugar on her fingers.

In Schleswig, there were no men. The Prussians had taken many of them for the army, or else they had fled from the Prussians to different parts of the world. A representative of the New Zealand government had travelled all over Denmark recruiting farm labourers for their skills with the axe. "You will clear the land first, then become farmers," he'd promised them. "And the women can work as servants, although they will most likely marry as there are many more men than women." The men left, and eventually the women realized if they wanted to find a husband they would have to follow them to the places to which they had gone: America, or Australia, or New Zealand.

When the war had taken the lives of her father and brother, she and

Maren had accepted an offer of free passage for young single women. Maren had wasted no time, meeting and marrying Pieter Sorensen on the boat between Hamburg and Napier, already pregnant with Hamlet by the time they disembarked in Napier.

Mette had moved in with her sister Maren and Maren's husband, but a second baby was on the way, and she probably would not be able to stay. Pieter had built her a little lean-to against the back wall of his and Maren's cottage, beside the lean-to where they kept the milch cow, but she knew with babies coming at great speed they would soon want her to leave, even if they didn't say so. They were kind, but it was time for her to find her own life.

Perhaps she could go to Wellington and find work. But she didn't want to work as a maid and she had no useful skills other than finding food in the bush, food that none of the other newcomers considered food. She didn't imagine anyone in Wellington eating huhu grubs or wetas when they ran out of meat.

Not that they ran out of meat these days. Mutton had become so cheap that even they could afford it - sixpence for a whole leg of mutton that would last them for most of a week, because all the sheep's wool was sent to England and something had to be done with the meat. But Pieter was saving every penny to put towards his farm, clearing the land and working at the sawmill as well. It was a hard life.

While the apron was drying, she'd planned to go into the bush behind the sawmill and find some food to supplement the cabbage, carrots and potatoes the settlers grew in among the tree stumps at the end of the clearing. They stored the vegetables in a covered pit, eking them out through the winter, but the store was almost empty, with planting about to start. Time for Mette to find another source, as much as Maren wished she would not.

Before she left, she prepared the camp oven, the heavy three-legged iron pot they used for cooking, building wood up under the flat pot and partly filling it with water from the butt. She would light the wood when she returned from the bush with food. The milch cow she had already milked this morning, and a fresh bucket of milk sat in the two-sided cupboard beside the front door, covered in a piece of heavy cotton cloth weighted down with stones sewn into the hem at the corners.

She tightened her bonnet around her head, pulling the strings into a slip knot under her chin, called out to Maren to tell her where she was going, stepped into her clogs and set off along the path through the bush to the sawmill. The path had been trodden down by the men from the clearing who walked to the sawmill every day at first light and back again as the sun was going down. She carried a large woven flax basket that she hoped would be full when she returned. The sun was nice, but she felt hot in her woollen skirt.

She was tall compared to most women she knew, too tall, with white blonde hair tied in two thick plaits, and hazel eyes. She knew she was not considered pretty, like Maren who had fluffy golden hair and enormous blue eyes. Once she and Maren had taken the tram over to Foxton to buy cloth for dresses, back when bullocks pulled the tram and it took forever to get to the coast. A young man in a dark suit had stared at Maren for a long time, and then had come up and said she was the most beautiful girl he had ever seen, and would she marry him?

Maren had looked calmly at the young man and told him she was already married, but suggested he might like her sister who had not yet found a husband. Mette had blushed, as she always did, and looked at the man, hoping he would understand it was a joke. Although she was embarrassed, she was prepared to laugh it off. But she was hurt and humiliated when the man looked back at her, dropped his gaze to the floor, and walked silently back to his seat.

"I'm suppose I'm not pretty enough for him," she whispered to Maren, although she was sure she was quite pretty enough for that man.

Maren had shrugged.

"What good does pretty do in this country? If he knew how you could cook he would come running back."

But a woman couldn't be too choosy, and Mette knew she was. She wanted to find a man who would give her healthy babies and make a home for her. But also someone who would enjoy talking to her beside the fire in the evening, someone who would be there when she looked up from her sewing. She imagined a sturdy, fair-haired man with a pipe in his mouth and a twinkle in his eye, a man who would talk to her about books and history and interesting things that were happening in the world. Danish men were not generally talkative types, however, and they certainly didn't fit the image she had in her head. Not any that she knew at least. On the other hand, neither did any of the other immigrants she had met since she arrived. They were a rough lot.

A group of young boys was playing in the dirt near the entrance to the bush. They stopped playing and looked at her with wide eyes.

"There's a troll in there," said one.

"In the bush?"

He nodded. His blond hair fell forward and he brushed it back. "We saw him. He was a big troll and he was holding a sack and a club."

Mette suppressed a smile. She'd seen just such a troll in a book of fairy tales when she was younger.

"And was he green with orange hair?"

One of the other boys jumped in. "No, he was brown and he had marks on his face, dark ones, like wings. And he had a big cloak made of feathers."

Well, that was a different kind of troll. Not the kind Mr. Anderson described in his stories, she thought.

"Why did you think it was a troll then?"

"Because he was angry," said the first boy. "He looked at us like he was going to put us in his sack and take us away for dinner. We were scared and we ran home."

Mette had nothing to say to that. But she felt a little twinge of nervousness in her scalp as she walked, as if someone was staring at her from the darkness of the woods. Once or twice she spun around to make sure she was alone. The troll sounded like one of the Hauhau Maren worried about.

The trees on the mountain side of the clearing were massive, larger than the span of a tall man; the bush was dark and full of things that were unknown to Danish people. She'd done her best to explore and understand the plants and animals, but knew she had much to learn. She forced her mind from the troll. The boys had imagined him, she was sure. They were boys. And boys had active imaginations.

She touched the leaves of a fuscia tree as she went by. Later in the autumn it would be covered with konini berries and she would make jam. Pieter loved her jam, and took a jam sandwich to work with him every day. Too soon for the berries yet, but she longed for something sweet. Savoury would be nice as well, something with taste, or bite, like the pickled herring they used to eat at home. On that memorable trip to Foxton on the tramway they'd visited a small café and she'd tasted whitebait fritters, made from the tiny fish that swam upstream in the springtime, cooked in a batter of eggs and white flour. She'd never tasted anything so delicious in her life, and she longed to taste them again.

Perhaps she would find some honey today. Manuka scrub flourished at the edge of the forest and was beginning to flower with small white buds. Bees loved the pollen from the manuka blossom. She stopped to pull off some leaves for tea, just the smallest and softest leaves, and tucked them carefully into one side of her basket in a kerchief placed there for just that purpose. The larger leaves made a bitter tea but the smaller ones were refreshing and you could almost imagine you were drinking real tea. If she could not find any honey she would at least have some leaves for tea.

She could hear the hum of the sawmill in the distance and as she got closer she thought she recognized the voices of Pieter and Hans Christian. Behind the mill a stream surrounded by fern and the occasional kowhai tree, not yet in bloom with its lovely yellow flowers, rose towards the hills and she climbed towards it. She pulled out some young fronds of pikopiko and put them beside the leaves. The roots tasted horrid, but they filled you up when you were hungry. Someone had suggested to her that pikopiko tasted like asparagus, but not to her. You might as well say that huhu grubs tasted like chicken, which they certainly did not. Ugh!

She wandered slightly off the path, being careful to keep it in sight. People were always disappearing into the bush and not coming back, especially small children, and she knew she must stay within sight of the path. Maren had put the fear of God into little Hamlet, telling him that the troll would get him if he went too far from the cottage. So far it had worked, although it had also made him nervous about going to bed at night, and he often woke in the night yelling that there was a troll under his little truckle bed. When that happened Maren and Pieter would take him into their bed. Maybe the other mothers in the clearing had told the same story to their boys and that was why they were claiming to have seen a troll. It was their name for a scary being who lived in the woods.

Still in sight of the clearing she found a large growth of puha, which would do for their vegetables. The leaves of puha, which was a type of thistle, were quite tasty if they were twice cooked in water—almost like spinach. Beside the puha were some red capped toadstools. She had avoided mushrooms and toadstools so far; you never knew which ones would kill you. She knew for certain that the red capped toadstools were not to be eaten. They made you go crazy, and then they killed you. She'd seen it happen with her own eyes.

A small sound made her turn and look to one side. A pair of bright eyes regarded her through the undergrowth. She stared into them and drew in her breath.

"*Hej min lille mand,*" she said softly, moving slowly towards the baby pig.

How they would love her if she came home with a little piglet for dinner!

She glanced down, looking for something heavy and spotted a hand-sized rock. Keeping her eyes on the pig, she bent and picked it up. The pig kept looking at her, its head on one side enquiringly. She took a minute to look around. If the mother was nearby she would run like a hen with its head chopped off to the clearing, but she knew baby wild pigs could become separated from their mothers and she would have heard a large wild pig moving through the bush. She hoped so, at least.

The little pig moved towards her slowly, a conspirator in its own death. It was busy nibbling leaves from the very puha she had just harvested when she raised the rock in two hands and brought it down hard on the side of its head. It fell slowly sideways, its eyes glazing over. To make sure, she hit it hard two more times, being sure not to get any blood on her woollen dress and stockings. Then she carefully lifted it and placed it in her basket. It was heavier than it looked and would give them so much meat! She covered it with leaves to keep the smell from the mother if she were nearby, turned, and walked towards home, the pig weighing her down on one side. She had trouble keeping from laughing. A pig for dinner. It would last them for days, and the fat under the skin would sizzle and cook into the most delightful taste. She could already imagine it.

After only a few steps she heard another noise, muffled steps in the leaves. She stopped. The mother pig was behind her. Now she was in trouble. She moved around carefully to see what was there. In the mottled shadows, she could not see well, but the pink skin of a pig would stand out against the green. Instead, she saw something brown. Some legs. Human legs. She raised her eyes and saw another pair of eyes looking down at her from under a blue cap, eyeing her in a way that was not unlike the way she had eyed the pig.

She gasped and almost dropped her basket. The troll.

A huge, dark-bearded man wrapped in a feathered cloak stared at her from the bush; or, more correctly, not at her but at her basket. He carried a bag of something that was moving, wriggling to get free, and she thought in horror of little Hamlet, wondering if he was safe at home. This was one of those Hauhau who ate little children. He was the troll the children had seen. The women in the clearing talked about the terrible Hauhau and scared the children with stories to make sure they behaved properly, often calling them trolls. She had not made the connection.

He raised his arm towards her and pointed at the basket. His face, the part that was not covered by his beard, bore blue markings resembling a large butterfly.

"*Poaka*," he said and snapped his fingers at her. She understood what he wanted. He wanted her pig. She backed away slowly.

"This is my pig," she said. "My *poaka*. For my family." She waved a hand towards the clearing. "They wait for me, over there. Many men. Big men." She heard her a quiver in her own voice and dug her nails into her hands to calm herself.

He shook his head dismissively. "My pig," he said, taking a step towards her. His voice was deep and gravelly, and sounded rusty, as if he didn't use it much.

She was still holding the rock she had used to kill the piglet and without thinking she threw it hard at his head. He grunted and took a few steps backwards, his hand to his forehead.

Clutching the basket with the pig close to her chest, she turned and ran, screaming loudly as she did so. She heard branches snapping behind her, expecting at any minute he would grasp her by the shoulders and seize the pig, but nothing happened. Even in her panic she realized that running back to the clearing would not help - there were no men there - so she ran towards the sawmill, which was a mere hundred or so yards away. She had the sawmill in sight and could even hear the machines running and men shouting, when a rider on a large black horse appeared in front of her on the track to the sawmill. It was him, she was sure, a big dark man with a blue cap, but for some reason he now wore a long blue-grey greatcoat which came down to his stirrups. She didn't stop to think about why he had changed his clothes, or how he was suddenly riding a horse, but opened her mouth and screamed as loudly as she could.

"What the dickens?" he said, clutching the reins of his horse as it reared up.